Parmenas Taylor Turnley, Cinderella Livingston Turnley

Private Letters of Parmenas Taylor Turnley

Parmenas Taylor Turnley, Cinderella Livingston Turnley

Private Letters of Parmenas Taylor Turnley

ISBN/EAN: 9783743389502

Manufactured in Europe, USA, Canada, Australia, Japa

Cover: Foto ©Raphael Reischuk / pixelio.de

Manufactured and distributed by brebook publishing software (www.brebook.com)

Parmenas Taylor Turnley, Cinderella Livingston Turnley

Private Letters of Parmenas Taylor Turnley

PRIVATE LETTERS

OF

PARMENAS TAYLOR TURNLEY,

(TOGETHER WITH SOME LETTERS OF HIS FATHER
AND GRANDFATHER,)

ON THE

CHARACTER OF THE CONSTITUTIONAL GOVERNMENT OF THE UNITED STATES, AND THE ANTAGONISM OF PURITANS TO CHRISTIANITY, &c.

Collected, Arranged, and Printed for Private Circulation only,
among Relatives of the Family,

BY HIS SISTER,

CINDERELLA L. TURNLEY.

LONDON:
PRINTED BY HARRISON AND SONS, ST. MARTIN'S LANE, W.C.

1863.

PRIVATE LETTERS

OF

PARMENAS TAYLOR TURNLEY,

(TOGETHER WITH SOME LETTERS OF HIS FATHER
AND GRANDFATHER,)

ON THE

CHARACTER OF THE CONSTITUTIONAL GOVERNMENT OF
THE UNITED STATES, AND THE ANTAGONISM OF
PURITANS TO CHRISTIANITY, &c.

Collected, Arranged, and Printed for Private Circulation only,
among Relatives of the Family,

BY HIS SISTER,

CINDERELLA L. TURNLEY.

LONDON:
PRINTED BY HARRISON AND SONS, ST. MARTIN'S LANE, W.C.

1863.

PRIVATE LETTERS

OF

PARMENAS TAYLOR TURNLEY,

(TOGETHER WITH SOME LETTERS OF HIS FATHER
AND GRANDFATHER,)

ON THE

CHARACTER OF THE CONSTITUTIONAL GOVERNMENT OF THE UNITED STATES, AND THE ANTAGONISM OF PURITANS TO CHRISTIANITY, &c.

Collected, Arranged, and Printed for Private Circulation only,
among Relatives of the Family,

BY HIS SISTER,

CINDERELLA L. TURNLEY.

LONDON:
PRINTED BY HARRISON AND SONS, ST. MARTIN'S LANE, W.C.

1863.

.˙. It is desirable this should *not* reach any American Official. ✓

INTRODUCTION.

A NATION which uses involuntary labour strives more to
"*preserve*" than to "*acquire*;" while, a nation using only
free labour, strives more to "acquire" than to "preserve."
Commerce, more than all else, tends to unite nations.
It makes them, step by step, dependent on each other,
and therefore, it makes them friends. One community
needs to buy that which another creates; while the latter
needs to *sell* what the former does not have nor create.
Hence, commerce is progressive,—the small beginning
leads to the moderate,—the moderate to the great,—the
great to the greatest; and, so long as the *principle* of
mutual exchange or interchange is observed, communities
or nations thus dealing with each other are friends, and
are united by strong ties of mutual good-will. But, not
so with *individuals* in a commercial community. The
spirit of commerce makes *enemies* of *individuals* in the
same community. More especially is this the case where
the same people or nation are plainly divided into two
distinct classes of vocations—one being purely commercial, the other being purely agricultural, or creative.
Wherever a people move *only* by the spirit of trade (or
commerce), they soon learn to make a traffic of the most

worthy of all human virtues! This is not only to be regretted, it is absolutely shocking, but none the less true. We have thus seen in the history of nations— purely commercial—that even the smallest dues of humanity are to be obtained for a price; and are, in fact, an article of commerce. It is true, the sense of trade which commerce (left alone) produces in the minds of its votaries approaches a very high sense of *exact justice*. That is, they will never *rob* outright, nor outside of a *rule of trade*. Neither will they ever contribute *charity*, nor stop to think for a moment of the *necessities* of any other class of humanity, *unless* such consideration comes within their commercial rule, and will benefit the trade. On the other hand, a community or a nation purely agricultural, or one to which *trade* is either unknown or prohibited, may rob outright, yet such community may have high regard for moral virtues, and may *favour* and *practice* the most charitable intercourse with each other, and with other communities. Hence we find that *hospitality* is much more rarely met with in commercial cities and marts of trade, than in the most remote frontiers, even, of a rude farming people.

In the collection of letters which follow, this characteristic of the distinct classes of people composing the United States is set forth. And also the tendency of the two classes of people in opposite directions as regards the American form and system of Government.

The North-Eastern or Puritan States of America have never given much thought to the mere *preservation* of any established system, but have looked almost entirely to acquisition, either of wealth, numbers, or physical development. On the other hand, the purely agricultural States have always given mainly their attention to *pre-servation*, letting any increase or acquisition be of secondary consideration. This spirit, in the two classes of people was and is *pre-existing*, and is independent of every accidental cause. But both tendencies have been, and are yet, constantly strengthened by the vocations or pursuits each respectively adopted. That is, the spirit *to acquire* in the North has been constantly increased by the food it lives on, which is, and ever has been, commerce and manufactures; while the spirit to preserve, and not to acquire, in the South, has been as constantly growing, by reason of their purely *creating* or agricultural pursuits.

For half a century the North has been purely free labouring; while the South has been using mixed labour, that is, part free and part slave labour. The slave labour thus used is that of the African heathen (to the manor born, though the descendant of the imported African of the last century). About one-fourth of the labourers in the South are the African; the other half being free, white Christians. A wise man once said that "the human family on earth appeared to be at war with each other;" but he did not tell us what the cause of this conflict or enmity is. Every one is thus left to speculate on this *cause* of conflict, according to his own capacity to reason about such things; and, in exercising this privilege we hold to the theory that a constant strife exists in all countries, and all ages, between two species of occupation or labour; one class of people being *creative* only, the other transforming and exchanging only. Between these two, then, there is a conflict since the world began, and will be, so long as man continues to act on the stage. If man would live by his own labour, and not by that of another, this conflict would cease; but this will only be when the millennium shall break upon us. This remark is not meant to apply to guardians nor masters, nor to him who uses serf or slave labour; but it is meant to apply to those who seek to live off the products of others, who have no claims to their protection from want, and who try to divert into their own coffers an undue amount of the profits, to the detriment of the producer.

The present conflict of war and blood, going on in the United States is nothing more nor less than the last and final effort of a purely agricultural people to sustain themselves against a long-continued and systematic effort of a purely commercial and manufacturing people to *depress* the agricultural—curtail the agriculturalists' profits, and enhance those of the commercialists and manufacturer. This conflict had to come, one day, to America, just as it has come to all nations. Of course, a thousand causes are assigned for the conflict coming when and as it did, still the *true* cause is most generally lost sight of, at least by those whose personal interest blind the mind's eye.

The following letters were written at a time, and under circumstances which were most favourable to see things in a proper light, and while I was then too young to understand or feel much interest in the very important subjects treated off; yet, at a riper age, I have not failed to read them with great care and the liveliest interest. The proof of great sagacity and sound judg-

ment of the writer is now being daily exhibited to the
world, in the million and a half of soldiers under arms,
in deadly conflict in America, where all was peace and
quiet when these letters were written!

Twenty millions of people in one section are trying to
crush out, and *extinguish*, if possible, ten millions in the
other section! The existence of slavery in one section is
assigned as the cause of this blood! Yet the very North
people who thus assert slavery to be the cause, actually
brought it to America, used it as long as it was profitable,
and then sold it out to the Southern people, for value
received in gold! The same North people have continued to live on the sweat and blood of the Negro, in
the shape of most exorbitant tariffs and " coasting-trade "
perquisites for half a century; and now, when the owners
of those Negroes roused themselves to allow no further
exactions, this slave-labour becomes all at once very
odious in the eyes of those who were quite content to
use it—so long as they could abuse it! The *true friends*
to the African Negro—(*slave* or *free*)—are the Southern
people. I am a native of a Slave State, yet never owned
one; my family, for four generations back, were all
natives of Slave States, yet never owned them; personal
pecuniary interest, therefore, cannot be said to influence
my feelings one way or the other; and, in collecting and
printing the private letters of a brother, my only apology
is, that I desire all my family relatives—who are utterly
surprised at the colossal proportions of this most inhuman
and vindictive war, in which they are shedding their blood
freely—may also know some of the most distant but
secret motives which has prompted to its gradual com-

mencement for nearly half a century. My own opinion is, that so far from African slavery being the cause of this war, it has actually prevented it for twenty years! I most sincerely believe that, if the *whole* of southern labour had been white free labour, that they would have *rebelled long, long ago*, against the undue exactions of Northern cupidity, tariffs, and coasting dues; but the poor Negro having broad shoulders and a hardy constitution has been the quiet pack-horse; with none to take his part, his owner preferred to move along quietly, suffering the excessive exactions to fall on his slave rather than make complaints which might lead to open rupture. And the six millions and half of *non-slaveowners in the Slave States* also strove for peace for a quarter of a century. But this quiet conservative mass in the South have every one of them jumped to their own rescue when every species of imposition, every epithet that could be spoken and written in the North against the character of the Southern people have completely taken possession of Northern minds. The Southern Christians now see their danger and condition, and what greater dangers they have escaped by "*secession.*" Hence it was only the sweat and blood of the Negro that kept off the conflict. His sweat and blood would *again* bring a temporary peace, if the South would only acquiesce in Northern tariffs, Northern shipping dues, and Northern dictation, as to all legislation in *agricultural States,*—then would peace come to-morrow. On the other hand, if there were not a slave on earth; if there were nothing but the white free labour in the South, and the South yet *persist* in throwing off those tariffs, and claim to do her own legislation, then

will the war continue just the same.   Peace comes, either
by the agriculturalist yielding to Northern commerce and
manufacturing, or by defending itself to the death !

Nothing is truer or plainer than this; so think the
two hundred and eighty thousand slaveowners in the
South; so think *the six and half millions of free white
non-slaveowners in the South*, and who are filling the
armies of the South in defence of (not slavery) but their
homes and firesides, and the dearest rights of Christian
souls—be he bond or free—black skin or white ! Never
in the history of the world had a people more cause to
call upon the Great Eternal for support, than the Christian people of the Southern States have at this time.
Never in the age of Christian warfare have any people,
army, or leaders, so utterly set aside the mitigated rules
of civilized and modern warfare as the Puritans have
done in this present conflict.   Women and innocent
children in villages and towns (whose husbands, fathers,
and brothers are ascertained to be in the Confederate
armies) are at once subjected to the most brutal treatment and gross insults by Federal officers and Federal
soldiers ! These helpless ones have *in thousands* been
given *one hour* only to leave their houses; and then, at a
few hundred yards distant, saw the same committed to
the flames by *Federal Puritan* officers.   Is not this
evidence of a religious (alas! not Christian) zeal, rather
than of patriotism ?   Not only so, but numerous instances exist in the Border States when Federal Puritans
have got possession, that when a Southern man had a
wife who was Puritan, *she* has delivered her own hus-
band to the *Federals*, and has seen him executed in sight

of his own house! Mr. Prior Lee, of Missouri, is one case. Numerous instances exist of Southern wives (but who were of Northern Puritans) *eloping* with Federal Puritan officers, while wives of Southern birth and blood married to Northern Puritan men, have deserted their husbands in order to remain in the South and give aid to the cause of the South. We ask, then, what can be clearer than that this present conflict is one of *religious Puritan frenzy* against Christian *faith,* hope, courage, and perseverance?

While the Christian world is called upon to sympathise with *Poland,* and while they do find great cause to sympathise and even aid her, it is equally true that Christians in every clime may not overlook brother Christians struggling as men never struggled before! It will one day appear that a little African heathen slavery is the *excuse* only—not the cause of the American war.

Affectionately,

A Sister,

C. L. T.

PRIVATE CORRESPONDENCE

ON

AMERICAN GOVERNMENT.

LETTER I.

New Orleans, July 4th, 1846.

I ARRIVED here safely, expecting to meet my regiment, with which I shall proceed on to Mexico, to join the main portion of the army now leaving its camps on the Rio Grande for Monterey. I have read with care all you say in regard to the war* which seems now to be upon us, whether we are willing for it or not. I think I can well account for your warm expressions of approval of the course of the President and his administration. Your " Democracy" is enough to explain this, if nothing else. But I know you feel other and stronger reasons than mere party attachment in the just cause we have of complaint, and the great propriety of our enforcing our claims by arms, if needs be. Still, as an abstract theory, I am averse to war (not that I want to be a soldier in peace, and a citizen in war), but the more I study of war—its objects, aims, results, and effects—I am convinced that more harm than good comes from it always, and it should therefore be avoided.

* The war declared with Mexico, May 13th, 1846.

B

It is now some years since you treated me to a lengthy dissertation on the political character of the Government of the United States, in which, if I mistake not, you thought you proved it was not a War Government, and could not be, from its very constitution. Many other topics you treated of (as to its magnificent perfection), none of which views have I ever made answer to. You must not, therefore, because of my silence, suppose for a moment that I agreed with you, or that I believe the half you said on this subject.

I did, however, at your solicitations, as well as from personal inclination, devote myself to a more careful study of the "revolution of these colonies" (which I choose to call a rebellion), and I must insist, in justice to my convictions, that I am more than ever convinced of the improper motives which actuated the Northern and Eastern colonies in that matter, and that some of the more Southern people also finally acted from quite unworthy motives. To have said this at that time your grandfather would have called good and loyal doctrine; but my grandfather would have called it Toryism, or traitorous, and it would not have been easy for one to escape rough handling. At present, however, I express the sentiment under the ægis of a free government. May be I shall always be able to do so; yet I must confess I am not without serious doubts on this point.

It did not require your hint that some of my political views are distasteful to you and to my grandfather. I am quite ready to believe that both of you will condemn much of what I express as my firm convictions of truth. But you call forth my views by your unasked animadversions, and I believe that you would prefer to know my honest feelings in the matter, rather than any "whitewashed" defence of what I do not believe to be true.

Hence, I trust to your magnanimity at least to give me credit for honesty of purpose. Neither can you attribute my views to any hostile feelings for our present magnificent country, because it is needless for me to assure you that no one living can enjoy its greatness, its blessings, and its liberty, more truly than I do. It is not, therefore, the present, nor the real, but that which I think to be perishable and false, that I so despise, and which I think permeates the whole structure. I do not see the evidences of continued advancement and prosperity which appear so plain to your mind's eye. Neither do I say that the defects I perceive are entirely in our system of government, although it has defects which will not fail to come to light from time to time. My fears are founded on something further back, and which had deep root long before our Government had any existence. It is in the very nature of men and of races, wherein I discover an utter want of homogeneousness, a direct antagonism, which holds the seeds of its own destruction. These seeds, of course, exist in all Governments; but all other Governments (with one or two exceptions) have provided for such evils, and take measures to prevent the evil tendencies. Our mother-country, England, for instance, had her streets drenched in blood before she discovered the real character and existence of these elements. But she has well provided for their control. Now, you will at once say that my views are those of all others who have no faith in popular government. Not so; I even differ from them also, as I will take occasion to show hereafter, as time will permit. Meanwhile, I hope you will all, in Tennessee and elsewhere, check the present symptoms of opposition to the war, and will give your hearty co-operation to the administration, in prosecuting it to a propitious end. Peace will not come in a day, or a week, but will in the course of a year or two, and when it does, I have no doubt but that our territorial limits (which you think are already sufficiently extended) will be still more enlarged.

Affectionately yours,

PARMENAS.

LETTER II.

Matamoras, August 12th, 1846.

I ARRIVED here two days ago, after a pleasant voyage— at least, as pleasant as could have been expected. I also find yours of the 15th ult. here a-head of me. I thank you for your promise to read my views on the subject of Democratic Government, a subject which you and grandfather think I know nothing about. Well, 'tis very likely I don't; but I think few do. Hence, I am the more willing to express my views, knowing that I will always have company in ignorance. There is a great difference between truths and what people think are truths; so is there between what we really know and what we think we know. Now, when I have all the surrounding facts before me, and the same evidences of results that others have, I cannot see why my inferences should be so wide of the mark as you would seem to pronounce even in advance. My opinion is, that your mind has been led to wrong conclusions because of wrong premises; and it will be my first effort to show this, and place, instead, correct premises.

In the first place, father, you are honest in your devotion to the best interest of the whole country; and hence you naturally suppose that all other people are also honest. Whereas they are not, nor the half of them. Secondly, you think all democrats are alike—hold like views, and aim at like results. This is also very erroneous. Thirdly, you look upon the Northern people and the Southern people as homogeneous and similar in manners and customs, and requiring similar laws; and you also look upon the democratic government in each as similar, and tending to like results; which I also assert is very far from being the truth. Now, much of your confusion in this matter results from what you understand to be a " democrat." You profess to be a " democrat " in the true sense of the term. You have allowed certain questions of legislative policy to direct you in choosing which side you would belong to; and that side having (by accident) taken the name of " democrat" in your State,* you class yourself and all men as democrats who oppose the general measures which you oppose. As I have been raised in the same county with yourself, I must have some correct ideas of your democracy south. You have admitted this before, and I think we will not disagree now. I fully coincide with you in opposition to the electing of your Judiciary by the people, and for the same reasons; yet that was and is eminently a democratic measure, yet very properly opposed by the democratic party south. We have always been together on the scrupulous and literal adherence to the terms of the Federal Constitution, yet such strict adherence is so far anti-democratic because, when the popular voice thinks any established rules not the best suited to all, such popular voice can, on purely democratic grounds, override or set aside such provisions. This is the true character and tendency of democracy in the North; but I assert that you have little or no tendency of this kind in the Southern States of the Union. On the contrary, all purely democratic tendencies or practices in the United States

* A Southern State—Tennessee.

Government are to be looked for in the North and not in the South. There is even some evidences of this difference in all the great questions of a political nature which have been discussed in the national councils for half a century, during which you and grandfather were lookers-on at events as they transpired, whereas I have come in as a mere dreamy reviewer of the records.

Now, in these records I find bank and anti-bank (I mean a national bank as a fiscal agent) and internal improvement by the general Government (instead of by the States or by private corporations). The holding public lands, and the Government being a kind of agency to peddle them out at so much the acre, instead of a general donation to the needy and the willing for homesteads; high tariffs on imported goods to aid and assist a class to build up similar manufactories in the east, *versus* a tariff for national revenue only ;—in all these matters you and I have always agreed. You called yourself a democrat; hence I also, in your estimation, must be a democrat. You opposed a bank; you opposed the peddling out of the lands, on pecuniary grounds, and favoured (on pecuniary, not democratic grounds at all) the giving away to actual settlers homesteads, because the enhanced value of revenues by the rapid settlement would be tenfold greater than the dollar or two per acre, with all the expenses of surveying and taking care of such a land-agency on the part of the Government. Also, you opposed specific tariffs, and you admitted that I gave you the clearest and best mathematical demonstration of its unfairness you ever had.

So far, then, we have been together. I have been thus particular in defining our positions, because I want to prove to you that I am, and ever have been, just as good and sound a democrat, in your sense of that word, as you are yourself; and yet I most emphatically assert that I am not a democrat in what I call the American sense of democracy. Athens had her democracy, and had her end too; Greece had her republics, mistaken, too, somewhat for democracies. The United States has democracies within her limits, and also republics; which I shall prove. The former are in the North; the latter are in the South. The Southern States are representative republics; the Northern States are the same only in name, but in practice the Northern States are democracies. It is this difference which I shall treat of hereafter, and a difference which, to my mind, foreshadows the extreme of peril. But I go back far beyond this, and ground these differences in pre-existing differences of the North and the South people.

More anon.

Affectionately yours,

PARMENAS.

LETTER III.

Comargo, Mexico, August 20th, 1846.

I ARRIVED here yesterday on a small steamer which ran up this little creek from where it empties into the Rio Grande some three miles distant. I say a creek, though it is known as the "San Juan River." I am preparing to leave and overtake the army with Taylor, now *en route* for Monterey, but I shall be delayed in order to form part of an escort with a supply train. I find no letters from you; but I have one from uncle J. A. T., of Alabama, exhorting me in his methodistical style to do and to be everything that is very good, and especially to take Washington for my guide in religious as well as in military practices.

This is certainly kind and thoughtful in my uncle; but, if he knew how slim are the hopes of his brevet second-lieutenant nephew to attain to rank enough ever to mark out a future in the line ." militaire," he would have saved himself the time and paper. On the other hand, if he had a more clear idea of my dislike to exhortations and preachers, he would have cut short even that part of his letter. I have just passed outside of the " preacher-ridden " United States, and have got into a " priest-ridden " Republic, and I prefer to enjoy their luxuries separately. This matter of "preachers" has much to do with my ideas of " Democracies " and " Republics," and constitutes an especial element in the antagonism of races which I shall have much to say about. I hope I shall not be bored with sectarianism in advance, else I may say some unfriendly things. My notion is, that half the wars which have cursed the world were brought about by "preachers;" and, when a war does occur in which they have had no part (as in the present), they should be more than cautious to keep quite aloof from its conduct. Our officers and army generally here show evident signs of exultation in the unity and harmony which pervade our forces over and above that extant in our Mexican enemies, and in the magnificent power of the United States, as a nation, over distracted Mexico; yet, when I look back from the Rio Grande to Maine, and consider the extreme diversity of character, of interest, of aims, and efforts—in other words, the intense " antagonism of races " in their very origin, the terrific hatred which is only slumbering from motives of expediency, but which, like the volcano, will ultimately break out, I can scarcely participate in the exultation. I constantly ask myself the question, how many decades will elapse before the United States are in a like, or even worse condition than Mexico? This will come. The motive will be this inherent antagonism; the means, or channels for its execution, will be diverse, some of which will be different habits, customs, religions, moral ethics, but, especially, difference of geographical pursuits and pecuniary interests. The occasion, or time, will be when a hatred sufficiently intense shall have been generated by a war of ideas between these "Republics" and those "Democracies." Republics have one object, which is a very cautious exercise of democratic theories and privileges. Democracies have for their object the full exercise of whatever the *vox populi* (no matter how expressed) may decide. Democracies have in view the making of laws and constitutions as they progress.

Now, in reply to this, you will treat me to a dissertation on the philosophy of the age, the example of other nations, a common interest, not to say analogous habits, &c. But, that philosophy is more proof on my side than yours; while all nations constantly prove that none ever yet profited by the experience of previous ones.

Now, here is my starting point in the subject I have promised to write you on, as it respects our own Government, which is an inherent antagonism between the (two) distinct classes of the American people; and the effort to mould all into one common system will produce (as it always has) disruption.

The Southern Colonies of the present United States were settled primarily by a class of people fully imbued with the orthodox-church Christianity of the age, and notions whence they came. They were honest, punctilious, and scrupulous; some were the idle dependencies of respectable families; but all were gentlemen, whose ideas of wealth were not measured by dollars, but by the manner in which it enabled them to live, and the extent it enabled them to exert moral influences among their fellow-men.

Their cultivation and refinement were not superficial, but, as a general rule, thorough and deep; their study of civil Government was extensive, and their experience in the same greater than that of any other people who ever settled a new country. They were not inventive, but followed pretty much the established rules of their predecessors, and of tradition, both in Church and State, as well as in domestic economy. We might say they were a fiftieth remove from the Feudal order, and retained but the semblance of that mode of settlement and of living; everything about them go to indicate this character—the very manner in which they would mark out fields and plantations (called in this country haciendas or villas), and the way in which they would locate their dwellings, in some vast woodland or park, and their vocation, always agricultural and rural. Their habits were those most conducive to health and development, as well of the body as of the intellect, but not rapidly. They did nothing hastily or in a hurry; they were slow and deliberate to a fault; would prefer to consume a whole year in building a house rather than do it in a month. Now, these were characteristics, not of the age, nor the country, nor of circumstances, but were distinct in breed—pre-existing elements in nature; and all those having these characteristics have always, and will necessarily, congregate together, all extraneous obstacles being removed. All persons possessing these qualities were equals under the law and in the church; so, also, did a social equality exist on the basis of—first, Christianity; second, refinement; third, cultivation. All Christians had certain inalienable equal rights, independent of themselves, while totally dependent on themselves, did they attain to, or not, certain social equality. But the heathen was not the equal of the Christian in any respect, but was always made subservient to the Christian in every position of life; yet this heathen was always made the especial object of instruction, example, admonition. He was not driven away, nor even permitted to go away. His very hours of sleep, of labour, of rest, and of spiritual culture were made to come and go by the Christian rule of superiority. This was not, and is not, considered to be merely an accidental superiority, but a Divine superiority, ordained of God, and having for its end the converting of the heathen to the light and life of Christ. Hence, the Southern Christians did not settle in large cities, or towns, nor did they ever build large towns, but dispersed themselves over wide-extended country, comparatively distant from each other. Their pursuits were not commercial nor mechanical; their life was not spent neither in store nor counting rooms, nor mechanic shops; their minds were not occupied with bank stocks, nor losses, nor profits. All these pursuits and modes of living are utterly incompatible with the Christianisation of the heathen, and has been since the world was redeemed, as also destructive to God's government prior to the Advent. Every characteristic of the Southern Christians goes to show that their tendency was, and is, to rural life, and the implanting of like habits, tastes, and natures into the heathens around them.

The clearing of the forest, the ploughing, the seed-time and harvest, seems to be the one prevailing idea and effort. Agricultural pursuits seem to be not an accident of the people, but the very incentive which influence their resting-place; not a consequence, but an antecedent; and it was a part of the blood and life of the mother-country whence they came. They appear not to be entirely prodigal adventurers, neither exiles, but so many arms of the same body, each forming a digit stretched out to develop the new soil for the double purpose of Christianising the heathen, and to advance the Christian by new and fresh products of God's soil. And this we apply to all those settlers, whether of English, Irish, Spanish, or French Christians. Their parent countries did much to assist them, and receive ample rewards for their assistance to early emigrants, if not in money, yet in products, information, and Christian advancements.

A mutual feeling of friendship and interest was at once established. A feeling of mutual dependence existed between the colonies and mother-countries; and, while those countries received rich returns, no colonists ever advanced so rapidly in all the elements of wealth, power, and influence; nor anything to compare with the strides which Christianity has made among the heathen.

This country of Mexico is called benighted, and all that; but when I look at the heathen population which Cortez and Spanish Christians met with here, in 1520, and now look at the Church and the "Cross," I think much has been done, even though abuses exist, and selfishness has perverted the best means to not the best ends. So, too, when I look at nearly three millions of negroes in the Southern States, whose parentage were fresh heathens, transported thither, I feel a conviction that the civilisation, humanisation, and Christianisation of them has progressed amazingly, notwithstanding some apparent perversions, and misapplication of some of the means; of course, defects among fallible and finite men must needs be expected. True, both English and Spanish settlers have had the field for labour on earth. A boundless country, the finest the eye of man ever rested on, with the greatest variety of climate, soil, and physical diversity, all inviting, and receiving the most rapid settlement and development of a highly civilised and refined people; but, aside from all these advantages (which may be called God's work), these people have measurably fulfilled the command to " convert the heathen." And, while a peculiar mind may reason that not half so much has been done as could have been done, yet this is begging the general question.

Such, then, was the condition of the Southern colonies, including Mexico, from the first settlement until the incipient "agitation" of the subject of rebellion against the mother-country. From that date I note a falling-off from the advance of those colonies, which will be the subject of future letters.

Affectionately yours,

PARMENAS.

LETTER IV.

Mier, Mexico, September 6th, 1846.

I ARRIVED yesterday at this little town, twenty-five miles from the Rio Grande. It is of no special interest to you, except, perhaps, as being the place where the noted Mier prisoners were taken, in the earlier Texas Revolution (some of whom were shot by drawing of lots, and among them we had one or two blood relations). Only think, that in the present age, which men call enlightened, and filled with a spirit of liberty and liberality, in this age, I say, imagine, if you can, a people calling themselves Christian taking as prisoners other Christians for an effort to establish their own independence and government. And thus to draw lots, as to which man shall be shot! Well, such is human nature, and so will it ever be, or at least till the "Millenium" draws nearer than we have signs of just at present. In my last, from Matamoras, I gave you some ideas I have of the peculiarities of character of those who first settled the Southern colonies of the United States, and also to some extent this country. I have yet a word to say of them, in a so-called religious point of view. As a class they were generally Roman Catholics or of the English Church, with a few Huguenots. In their natures they were not inquisitive, not at all disputative, nor inclined to metaphysical dissertation either in Church or State. Little or no scepticism existed either in their religion or politics; plain maxims and established rules (whether good or bad) were closely followed without question or criticism. There was more than a mere absence of disputation; there was an absolute repugnance to it, and had its seat in their very natures, not in accidental surroundings or education, but pre-existed in this class of people. This pre-existing innate dislike to metaphysical discussion must not be overlooked, because it did then, and does yet, exist, and is the foundation of antagonism on the one side between the two classes I am going to treat of. The class just spoken of were not possessed of what one might call "restless energy," nor a disquieted temperament, but rather a deliberate, I may say, indolent: and entertaining an especially high regard for blood, lineage, race, and Christian culture with refinement, these were and are to this day ruling emotions in the breast of the people of the Southern States and of Mexico; praiseworthy notions, indeed, but where circulated as the only capital of certain degenerate descendants, it becomes, to say the least, very irksome. I am now going to leave the settlers of Southern soil to go on with their own affairs, their developments, their laws, rules, regulations; with all their attachments to the power and tradition of the mother-countries, none of whom as a class were exiles, or fugitives therefrom, but in reality were the petted children of a parent who almost watched for their return. Scarce an artisan or mechanic among them, and none inclined either to manufacture or commerce; but their whole united energies were turned to the rural life of agriculture, and their herds and flocks.

A constant and growing demand for labourers in the New World was also a relief to the crowded populations of the mother-country, who was liberal in bestowing large grants of land to selected persons, which thus kept the control of affairs in the hands of a comparatively small number, and thus insured more stability and harmony, but less democracy in the new Government. Just at this point, too, it is proper to place the origin of the present prevailing spirit of republican representative society in all the South rather than a spirit of broad democracy (which, I will show hereafter, prevails in the North). The control of public matters being thus delegated to a few well chosen agents, was the cause of much harmony, and while some corruptions are inherent to all human affairs, yet we may say, that, whatever of evil did exist in the South, it was more a violation of fixed rule than any compromise with it; and that, where honesty and virtue were lacking in public affairs, natural attachment to fixed maxims and rules served very much to avert the evils from society which might have followed. Besides the whole society being directed to one pursuit, and that the least favourable to the growth of views, there was less to be feared or guarded against either in morals, religion, or politics. The Bible holds out to us in all of its pages that the greatest virtues and fewest vices find place among the tillers of the soil. Profane history also has taught the same for thousands of years, and doubtless all who have had the opportunity of studying the different vocations in life will at once feel the truth of the idea. Great cities and ex-clusively commercial and manufacturing districts exhibit to our eyes the greatest chastity of manners, and by the side of it the deepest and darkest hues of vice and infamy. While the rural communities show less chastity of manners, yet accompanied with a most rigid virtue, the simplest, not to say rude habits.

At this period (1770) the Southern States were in their greatest prosperity, and, I may say, gave real evidences of Christian progress. We have no record of any people having enjoyed greater happiness, more peace, or made greater strides in the great work of converting the heathen to Christian faith, than did the people from New Jersey to Carolina in the United States and the Gatupins in this country. Especially Maryland, Virginia, the Carolina, and Georgia were the most prosperous and advanced because of their people. They had neither manufacture nor commerce, neither did they wish any, because, first, they were by nature averse to such pursuits and sought the quiet of agriculture instead; just as the heathen, to whom their mission seems to have been directed, preferred the far distant and lonely forest to the comforts of a civilised home.

They found in Mother Earth everything which nature required, and the excessive surplus procured for them the implements of husbandry, comforts, and refinement from the artizans of the mother-country. The colonists fed the world, and ships of commerce conveyed from and brought the articles to their very doors, while each class was pursuing the species of labour assigned them, yet working to each other's happiness and progress, and so far separate the while as to prevent interference. How strange that disruption should so soon follow it in 1776; still it did come, perchance not for ever. We will look at this hereafter.

Affectionately yours,

PARMENAS.

LETTER V.

Marina, Mexico, September 27th, 1846.

WELL, I have at last come to a halt for a time, in order
to repair wagons and all et ceteras which appertain to a
long wagon-train moving in our enemy's country. The
fact is, with proper energy and vigilance on the part of
the Mexican troops, these large trains could be cut all in
pieces in spite of guards,

My rank being that of second lieutenant, I can only
aspire to a kind of chief-wagon-master; but even in this
I am useful, and daily find opportunities to put in practice my early lessons in hauling saw-logs to the mill,
hauling rails to new ground, to say nothing of breaking
young mules and horses to the plough and wagons. Tell
grandfather, that if the colonies were as improvident in
their means for transportation in 1778 to 1780, as the
Government is at present, I have no surprise at the
national debt the country was obliged to pay after the
close of the Revolution. Wars cost money, which some
one must get, else there would be fewer of them. Taylor
had a fight at Monterey (20th to 23rd), took the city,
and holds it—which was to be expected; and that is all I
have yet learned on the subject.

The enterprising public press will doubtless give you
all the particulars, and doubtless a thousand times more
than is true, long before you receive this. A score or two
of penny-a-liners are following the army; whether for the
interest of the service in general, or only for the political
portion of it, I do not know.

An armistice was agreed upon at Monterey, between
General Taylor and the enemy, which is somewhat com-
plained of; but you had best not prejudge anyone—rather
wait till you hear both sides of the stipulation. An

C

armistice is the only mitigating feature of a bloody battle.

I closed my preliminary remarks on the character and habits of the first settlers of the Southern Colonies of the United States in my last letter from Mier, which is a small town about sixty miles from here; and I have jotted down since then some views respecting the other class of people which settled the North-eastern Colonies. I say nothing of New Jersey, Pennsylvania, Rhode Island, and Delaware, because they were not unlike those of the Southern Colonies; while in New York the classes were somewhat mixed. But whatever influence the Dutch exerted, it was with that of the surrounding, or what we now call Middle States. I therefore consider only and especially the New England settlements. I am also somewhat at a loss how to designate the class of New Englanders; for you and grandfather will at once accuse me of prejudice. Still I shall have so much to say in their favour (as the world now goes) that I will risk it.

The New England States, then, were settled about the same time as Maryland and Virginia, and therefore much earlier than the Carolinas or Georgia; but the emigrants were widely different from those we have heretofore considered. They were less scrupulous in forms, they ignored many of the established customs, and they aimed less at the shadow than at the substance. They were more prone to physical things, and less to moral and mental exercises. They were more active, and had more of what we call at this time energy; finding it exceedingly difficult to remain quiet, either in body or mind. Nature had not endowed them with any taste for the rural life of agriculture, nor with the patience requisite to rely upon the slow progress of the returns of the husbandman. The Southern colonists have sometimes been called Cavaliers, and those of the Eastern States Puritans; but neither is entirely correct. The Southern people are not and were not entirely of Cavalier origin, though it vastly predominated; nor were all of the New Englanders Puritans, though with them also the larger portion belonged to that branch. In fact, many of the characteristic traits of the two classes go back many centuries beyond the use of those terms. " Puritan" and " Cavalier" are, so to speak, of recent coinage; and I wish to speak of the character of both, rather than of any name which designate them. With this explanation, however, I will use the terms merely as a convenience, and not as embodying all of the elements, which is the object of my consideration. Perhaps a better religious division would be Puritans and Churchmen, because under these heads are best known the antagonistic elements which were first transplanted to this continent. By Churchmen I mean all who settled in the Southern Colonies — whether Catholics, Protestants, Huguenots, Quakers, or Baptists; and by Puritan I mean all who are in opposition to the former, whether on this continent or Europe, for the past two thousand years; because just here is the grand line of division between two classes; I make but the two divisions in the world, whatever be their country or clime, and I find the line of their demarcation in their creed or faith, or whatever you may call it. However subdivided people may seem to exist, such subdivision is only apparent, and not contradictory of my division. To illustrate this, God divides his creatures into two classes only (*i. e.*), those who love, fear, and serve Him, and those who do not. Now, as no living creature hath the power to decide who belongs to either, since every one professes to have the conviction that his class is the one, and, as no creature can separate himself from that to which he may by nature belong, to judge rightly, it would,

c 2

of course, be as futile as presumptuous for any one to attempt to explain the division which God hath made; still, without leaning to the practices of either, we may very properly consider the habits and characters of all men simply in two classes, without knowing or feeling an interest in either class; we may very properly consider the physical, social, political, and moral proclivities of all people, and thus (like assorting cards) throw them finally into just two classes. I hope you will not think there is any want of reverence in this, for certainly none is intended, nor is any felt. As we cannot know the secrets of each other's hearts, we have to rely on outward actions for the evidences (among men) of what is reverent or irreverent: hence, I do not wish you to construe these ideas of mine as indicating the one or the other. The visible physical traits and practices of these two classes are very different, and so they are all over the world, as well among heathens as among Christians. Some of these traits are so plainly visible on this continent that they need scarce be mentioned: hence, in the Southern people we find sloth, indolence, inaction, intellectual as well as physical culture, faith, hope, love, and charity— the extreme representation of order, system, rule, aversion to change or rapid motion, seeing, learning, and acting but few things (comparatively), and those very gradually and very thoroughly, always contending for a principle on which to base action rather than expediency.

Now, as a class, we find the New Englanders to possess elements of energy, activity, great desire for physical enjoyments, extreme proneness to change, no regard for rule, order, or system, great practical efforts regardless of theory, slight evidences of faith, no hope but of a physical kind, no love or charity, great restlessness, much impatience, and a sleepless vigilance, seeing, learning, acting, all things partially, and nothing thoroughly; always acting from expediencies rather than theory or principle, full of scepticism, which sets in motion great enquiry, which also results in much change and constant experiment. The foregoing characteristics of the two classes of people in our nation I believe to be correctly stated; I believe the same to be, not the consequences of any accidental, local, or educational causes, but the same innate, pre-existing elements which direct, control, and dispose of their respective vocations, places of abode, shape their institutions, and control their weal or woe on earth, and among the nations thereof: hence it is I discover, wherever these people have now and then intermixed, as it were, in the same community, hath general peace prevailed; but, where either predominated, war ensued; like opposite electricities in the same body, both being present to a certain extent, left the body in a quiet or neutral state; but, where either was in excess, agitation resulted. So, also, where they have not intermingled, but were so located as to forbid interference, yet have intercourse, then peace was the result; but, wherever a closer proximity and intercourse, then came conflicts: thus it is that I discover an utter impossibility of a peaceful Government with these two classes so nearly together. It is to me impossible, unless you could so intermarry the whole as to destroy a concentration of these antagonistic elements; but, as this intermarriage cannot be effected in many countries, if at all, I entertain no idea of a long duration of a peace; neither have I laid the causes of conflict in difference of customs, manners, or habits, or any real or visible difference in their religious or political views.

Although the difference in these respects will be the means of bringing it on, yet the prime first motive, as it were, lies in these first great different natures, which I call "antagonism of races." In subsequent letters I will more particularly consider the extent and bearing of the differences in political habits, social relations, and domestic economy of the two people, which must play a great part in future troubles; but all such differences are the results of the first antagonism, not antecedent.

Affectionately yours,

PARMENAS.

LETTER VI.

Monterey, Mexico, October 20th, 1846.

I HAVE been for ten days or two weeks at this place, and I feel somewhat rested from our long and wearisome march, though my health is by no means good, on which account, and my regiment a foot concern, I am half inclined to tender my resignation. This, however, would not look like aiding the Administration in the war. Still, the limited field that I am confined to, scarce gives aid to the cause, especially in the midst of such an army of high commissions in the political troops now pouring in (or I should say) volunteers or "sovereigns." Colonels, majors, and captains abound, with a few days' or week's experience in military matters, while I, in my fifth year can scarce boast of the lowest lieutenant's grade. These "sovereigns" look upon the "regulars" as a set of indolent pensioners on a glorious free Government, who are only fit for garrison duty at some retired or frontier post in time of peace, and good routinists for the brave and sagacious volunteers when war comes; and, in turn, the regular looks upon the "volunteer sovereign," with his spread eagles, as an impudent ass, good at political tricks, which generally culminate in war, the brunt of which the sovereign never bears.

I am glad to receive yours of the 25th ultimo, and thank you for your kind patient review of my remarks. I did not suppose that I should receive much favour at your hands in the way I treated the subject, and I have not been disappointed; I am one of those that expect nothing, and am therefore seldom disappointed; however, I will not argue these points here, nor attempt to answer your objections, but will allow you to have your own views. You can throw all my letters into that old desk at " Oak Grove Museum," where they will moulder away by time, as you say my theories will. But, of course, I do not believe one half you say. Before you get this you will have received and read another long letter upon the same subject, and it will, no doubt, be further evidence to your mind of my " aberration ;" but you must not infer that I give other signs of " insanity," or that the regimental surgeon has any apprehension for me on this point, because he and I take a " wee drap" together; besides, he is far behind me on our " whist docket."

I closed my last letter with a division of our people into two classes. I had previously considered some of the peculiarities of the Southern settlers, and I now wish to mention some of the characteristics of the New Englanders; because this is necessary, in order to properly consider the local differences of habits, customs, and political economy of the two peoples.

The first settlers, then, in New England were " Puritans," so called. They are, however, one of the classes already defined. Their extreme restlessness in the mother-country, constantly aggravated by not being allowed as great an influence and control in the Government as they desired, and not being sufficiently strong to obtain

it by the sword, they scattered over to Holland and elsewhere, and called themselves "the persecuted." Religious
persecution was the epithet they ascribed to the motive
which denied them all the political rights they thought
themselves entitled to in England. The same thing
occurred in other nations ; and it is proper for me to state
here, that the class I am treating of, whether you call them
" Puritans," or any other name, or whether you locate
them in New or Old England, or under the tropics, still
that class of people have, for three thousand years, always
considered all social and temporal affairs, and political
economy, as well as customs and manners, as being inse-
parably connected with religion, and that all their accidents
of life go to make up religion. Hence, a deprivation of
any, is, with them, a deprivation of religious enjoyment. A full enjoyment of all is their sum total of
religious joy. Now, I do not mean to say that they are
purely worldly and not spiritual in their religion. What
I intend to say is, that they are just as much so as their
natures admit of, and that they discover no distinction
between the various accidental relations and a religion;
and that whatever of spirituality there may be in it belongs
just as much to those accidents as to any other part of
their religion. This is surely the history of Puritans in
England, Holland, Poland, Austria, Russia, France,
Germany, and the United States.

Not finding Holland any more disposed than the English
Government, they at once procured grants from the
Crown, and set out for the New World, landing at
Plymouth Rock, an event still commemorated by them.
They speedily began to put in operation a social system to
suit themselves. Their whole customs were different from
those of the South ; they built houses differently ; they
ate, slept, and drank in a different manner ; they married,

and were buried differently; their labours were different; they settled in towns; villages and cities were soon built; commerce and the mechanical arts claimed their entire attention. They were not a creating people, but a handy, ingenious, " barter and exchange" people. They despised agricultural pursuits, because this was too slow a mode of acquiring wealth and influence. The commercial and mechanical were much more advantageous in this respect. They soon forgot their late hatred to English Church and State (if indeed they ever had any), because they at once organised civil government, with all the ecclesiastical incumbrances possible to conceive of, and buried all their enmity to the Throne and Parliament in exchange for good grants of land, and a liberal trade of the home people.

In this way their population increased every year by large emigration, though not fast, as Virginia, and the emigrants, whether from England, France, or Germany, were always of the class " Puritan," or some of the adjuncts. In fact, their first organisation was made to exclude all other sects or denominations. They were not even half as liberal as the Mother-Church, in which they had imagined they suffered great religious persecution, because deprived of some political or temporal power. They showed much less sagacity and sound sense in their civil policy than any people who have ever attempted to establish a government; but this is owing to the exclusive and classified nature of the people. They contained but one class of talent, and that of the purely material or physically inclined, all in pursuit of the same purposes, namely a speedy acquisition of wealth, with as little to do with surrounding tribes or people as would enable them to obtain the end they sought. A brisk trade speedily grew up between them, and the mother-country, but little or none for a long time between them and the Southern colonies. In fact, the two peoples were as distinct in intercourse as they were in natures. May I not express the fear that the blood of thousands yet to be shed will attest the great misfortune that they ever became better acquainted? The New Englanders were a very industrious and energetic people; such was and is their nature, and their natures directed them to a climate calculated to keep them so. They were excessively religious; whether it were of the Christian kind, I am not called upon to say. My own opinion is, that much blood will yet be shed for the sake of that which will still remain in doubt.

Their articles of traffic were, lumber in its various shapes, fish, and also some hemp and flax, which required but slight culture of the soil to produce. They soon commenced a more extensive system of manufacturing in other branches, and extended ship-building, showing that their very natures directed them' quite as much to their vocations and thence to the mercantile, as did the Southern people take to the soil. It is beyond doubt the pre-existing element, which first directed the two classes to their respective latitudes in the first place on this continent. The peculiar labours to which the New Englanders directed their minds called for a special class of emigrants each succeeding year, and as constantly drove away from them the heathen among whom they had settled, because the only species of labour which God seems to have vouchsafed to the Indian or heathen is that of the soil or chase, and they offered no assistance or inducements to pursue such in the North and East. So with the heathen African; he never found a field for labour with the New Englanders, nor did any other creature, unless he was mechanically or commercially inclined. Of course, I do not mean to reduce the assertion down to isolated individuals, but I speak of a class. This remark holds good in all nations and ages with respect to the class, of which the "Puritans of America" are a very small part. This class of people the world over have never mingled with the heathen nor converted any to the Christian faith.

The critic will, of course, instance numerous missionary societies organised by this class. As a proof that my statement in this respect is a correct one, I will only ask you to trace carefully these efforts to their end, and I think you will agree with me. I will now leave the New Englanders to pursue their trade and develop their resources and country up to the incipient stages of the rebellion against the English Government (1760 to 1775).

I shall then consider both classes together, as they had by that time formed considerable business relations, and had made many efforts, not entirely unsuccessful, to unite discordant elements centuries old, and to mould into one homogeneous element natures very dissimilar. I think these natures cannot be amalgamated into one. I also think, the attempt to do so has been going violently on in this nation since 1765 up to the present time, but without effect, and I think a continuance of the same effort will convulse this nation, perhaps the whole continent, or even Europe, and still be unaccomplished. I shall then in other letters point out some of the physical elements, political and pecuniary differences, as evidences of a first, greater, and pre-existing difference, as well as to show, that these physical, visible, differences will be the agents or means which will lead to this deplorable result.

Affectionately yours,

PARMENAS.

LETTER VII.

China, Mexico, Nov. 1st, 1846.

I ARRIVED here a few days since, having performed the circuitous travel from Monterey down to Camergo, and thence across to this little town of "Arenges-dulcy," or, as the Spanish say, "Naruncas de China." This people and country present to my mind a strange spectacle of freedom and indolence, the latter obviously the consequence of the former. Yes, I assert that this indolence is a consequence of freedom. The truth is, there is no element in Government so erroneously understood, and so ruinously interpreted of late years, as that of freedom. The enjoyment of certain inalienable rights is surely the proper, if not the only object of Government. But there are those in the world (and of such this country is filled) whose ideas of liberty is exemption from labour—either physical or mental. Nor is it strange that such should be the prevailing sentiment here, since the people are a partially civilized Indian, by a cross between the original heathen, and the Christian Castilian; yet Mexico, by her haste to imitate America—in theory, achieved her political independence from Spain, without a single preparation in the character or manners of her people to understand, appreciate, or enjoy the social relations it was meant to secure. This is a representative Republic; but there is nothing for the "Deputodus" to represent but crude, half savage ideas of—liberty from labour and effort. Not a liberty to push forward in the great field of human development, but a liberty to push back into indolent sloth, and quiet inaction. Query, hath not some of these false ideas of liberty come from those extremely metaphysical expressions in the Declaration of American Independence, such as, "All men are created free and equal."

This expression is true only in a certain abstract sense. It is false in all respects of practical application, in which it strikes the ordinary mind. Question second, Was it not meant to be a cunningly devised truth, in the abstract dressed in practical falsehood, to do much harm? I think, whether meant so or not, such is, and has been, and will still be the practical effect. Undoubtedly such is the broadcast effects here in Mexico. If I chose to dissect that broad assertion, I could easily show its absurdity, if not utter falsity, because everything on earth, and I might say in heaven, will bear witness to the fact that all men are not born equal, nor free, nor created equal; indeed, the very opposite is more nearly true, *i. e.*, all men are born bondsmen, and unequal in temporal conditions, mental faculties, and physical forms. However, I will not pursue this subject further than to assert the fact that this so-called Republic of Mexico is early feeling the bitter fruits of attempting to put into practice an impracticable theory, whether possessed of abstract truth or not. The attempt, merely, to amalgamate into one homogeneous mass, elements and characters utterly discordant and diverse, has proved a sad failure in Mexico. It is for wise statesmen to see to it, that a like failure does not occur elsewhere Forcing the Christian on a par with the heathen, rather than forcing the heathen gradually up to a par with the Christian ! A levelling down, instead of a levelling up; but, such is the object of the theory, because it is much quicker to level down than to level up. It is easier to rake down the hill than to carry the earth and fill in the depression. So with society, it is easier to force an equality on paper, than to develop an actual equality by time and diligent development of natures and manners. Mexico is not the only people who will yet suffer the evils of such theories. The truth is, I don't believe the reputed

author of the words I have quoted (Jefferson) really
believed the truth of the assertion; but he uttered the
same under pressure, and the ambitious impulses of the
occasion; either this, or else he meant it to apply only to
men in a Christian sense; and this takes me back to the
people and the period at which I closed my last letter
(from Monterey), which I trust you have received before
this; I closed that letter about the incipient stages of the
rebellion of the American colonies, and I am going to
pursue the subject thenceforward, by treating of both
classes of peoples. I am sorry that I am without some
books of dates, places, and events, but, such are not
essential for my purposes, because I am not attempting
to write a history, nor to prove any fact; I am only giving
my own convictions of facts—past, present, and yet to
come; and whatever events or circumstances I note in
this connection are only referred to as showing my grounds
for belief. About 1760 I think we may note the incipient
spirit of rebellion, and it began, as all revolutions have for
three thousand years, among the " class " inhabiting the
New England States. I do not say among the New
Englanders, I say among that "class." I do not say this
in any unfriendly spirit; I say it because it is a fact. If
the act, or acts, were commendable, then they receive the
praise. If not, but were reprehensible, then they will
receive the odium. I pass no judgment on the merits or
demerits of the spirit which began that, and all other
rebellions since Moses; they may all have been right, and
may have resulted in good, or the reverse. I only assert
that the class of mankind to which the New England
Puritans belonged, did actually begin, and carry on, and
nurture a spirit of rebellion against the mother-country
from about 1760 till 1776, when they succeeded in inducing
all other of the colonies to join them. The ostensible

object of that rebellion, too, was to get rid of taxation ; to get rid of import, export, and excise taxes, stamp taxes, &c., &c. This, I say, was the ostensible or avowed object; and it is the only acknowledged grounds on which such rebellion could ever have received the assistance of colonies south of New York. But I deny that such was the real grounds. I have not time to go into the secret springs of the Parliament, and see how many of the same class there aided and assisted in imposing those taxes on to their Puritan brethren in New England States, for the express purpose of creating a disruption. But such was a well-digested plan, and had a double object in view, only one of which succeeded, and that but half way. First, it was the plan to replace the English Government in the hands of a second Cromwell; secondly, to place the American colonies under the same control, but with a separate seat of government. Now, this was the actual, hidden motive of all the New England States, together with their co-religionists in Europe, elsewhere as well as in England. But such motive was carefully veiled under the garb of resistance to taxes, and burthens which were palpable and visible to all, and alike repugnant to all, and therefore commanded the approval of the very opposite class. Hence, the New England States raised the flag of resistance to taxation, under which to recruit; and she succeeded. She soon went one step further, and got a Confederation of States. (A little later she took another step, and got a consolidated Government—not quite, but she came as nearly succeeding as it was possible. Had New England logic affected Patrick Henry, and a few others, as it did Madison, and some other Southern statesmen, then would a consolidation been complete). There is an unwritten history of the efforts of the New England States (from 1760 to 1775, a period of fifteen

all countries. No doubt grandfather can recollect most of
it which occurred in Virginia. Governor Bottetourt* (after
whom grandfather's native county is named) left a record
of those times which is known to some yet living. New
England outwardly and ostensibly wanted to get rid of
undue taxes; but New England wanted, really and secretly,
a religious democracy, and wanted to control and manage the
commercial and manufacturing interests of the New World;
while New Englanders in old England were working at
the same pump-handle in that country. New England
people did not care so much for a few taxes; they did
not think it so much burthen to supply a little fuel and
some comfortable barracks to a few Royal troops. They
did not think a few revenue cutters, or a few ship-loads of
tea of such vast importance as to want blood solely on
that account. No! these were the means to convert
others to the cause, while the motive was to be kept concealed till the proper time. That proper time will yet
come. It will be when the whole public mind is directed
to something else, or else is steeped in incredulity, and is
under the rule of a "dominant democracy."

To show how the Southern colonies first doubted the
propriety of that rebellion, I will mention the fact that
Governor Bottetourt, of Virginia, actually dissolved the
House of Burgess, because they merely received a petition
from the State of Massachusetts, urging resistance to the
laws of Parliament! Maryland did the same, and North
Carolina the same, until the same colony and South
Carolina were filled with agents from the New England
colonies in disguise (pretending to be citizens of the
Southern colonies), who were engaged on the borders and
interior creating disaffection, by forming bands of "free-

---

* He was the Governor the King had appointed over Virginia.

booters," to pillage, and then "regulators," to pursue and
detect them. By this means two parties were formed in
those Southern States (or colonies), one for, the other
against, the Governors, who were Crown officers. A band
of these imported New Englanders would commit robberies
which it was the business of the Crown officers to ferret
out and punish; but some of the same parties had previously arranged to be the agents and servants of the
unsuspecting Governors in detecting the evil ones, and
which, of course, therefore failed. Hence the common
people soon began to lose confidence in the Governors and
officers, which was speedily followed, of course, by a
general democratic deposing of those officers and those of
their own (a New England selection) placed instead!
Such is my reading of the unwritten history of those
times, without bias, partiality, favour, or affection. These
efforts were successful; a Declaration of Independence
followed six or seven years of war; then a peace of arms
in the field, but a war of ideas in the legislative halls
which hath never ceased. Now, I do not excuse or approve
of the course pursued by either King or Parliament. The
King certainly was a mixture of weakness and wickedness;
while the Parliament acted more like men who had lost
all sense of reason, and were governed more by a madness precedent to destruction than like legislators or philosophers. Such madness alone was necessary for their
defeat. Still, unwarranted as were the acts of King and
Parliament after war commenced, this was no excuse for
the equally unwarranted acts of New Englanders in
mobbing soldiers, burning vessels, throwing overboard tea,
ordering royal troops out of their cities and districts,—all
which acts were actually revolutionary and disloyal by
intent and preconceived plan, and not solely to redress
the slight wrongs set up as the reasons for it, but actually

D

for a power beyond that—and outside of all, even far
beyond the expectation of the Southern colonies, which
were fast becoming her allies,—under a false impression
of the objects in view. Hence it is, father, that I did, a
few years ago, express to you my firm conviction that
the secret, hidden, and unrevealed motives of that rebellion made the same a crime, the punishment whereof is
yet to be inflicted on the American people! The bitter
fruits of that subterfuge, hypocrisy, and deceit did not
ripen during that Revolution, nor since, but will in due
course of time, and will be pressed to the lips of many
generations of those who thus deceived and were deceived.

I do not oppose revolution in certain specific cases of
necessity; but I assert that no such necessity did then
exist in fact. Happy for us that, in our present Government, we have tried at least to lay the foundation for a
political revolution instead of a bloody one. In the
monarchical Government of England no such provision
existed. The world, even, had no knowledge of a peaceful
or political revolution; and to this extent we have to
excuse the silly, wicked course of both King and Parliament. Such coercion as they persisted in, if practised by
our own Government at this day, against any one or more
of the States, would be more diabolical than was the act
of England; and, I will add, would be the perfect proof
of my views on antagonism of races, since it would
prove that Governments, laws, and constitutions are
nothing; but that habits, manners, customs, hatred and
revenge is all in all. That is, that democracy is just as
tyrannical, and more so, than Kings and Parliaments.
However, in reply to all this, you will account me a fool,
or, at least, a visionary dreamer, and will, doubtless, beg
the question by asking me, what a miserable set of serfs
and slaves we would all have been had we not carried

forward that great revolution, and established this great, free, popular Government. You will thus speak because you really thus think and feel. You see nothing but what is good and lasting in this new Government. Happy you are, too, in thus seeing. I do not thus view it, and hence would not be happy were I not more philosophical. Your faith serves you, my philosophy serves me. So must it be.

I have offered you no proofs of what I have asserted. I have only stated what I have gleaned from study and observation as satisfactory proofs to my mind. The New Englanders I believe to be of that class which constitute the revolutionary elements of the world; and that wherever a sufficient number of them get together, with a sufficient opposing force in their reach, a revolution is sure to follow. That these opposing elements are inherent and are antagonistic, and have been for thousands of years; but the channels through which this antagonism has been, and is at present, and will continue to be, made manifest, can be clearly pointed out. It is seen all over the world; but that only in our own country will receive my comments or notice. Hence, to consider these channels, we go back to the primitive division, and start at their physical diversities in worldly pursuits. The revolutionary class being commercial, manufacturing, trading, bartering, exchanging, and banking, active, restless, and vigilant. The other agricultural, being naturally peaceful, lawful, patient, enduring and suffering, slow and indolent.

More anon.

Affectionately yours,

PARMENAS.

LETTER VIII.

Victoria, January 20th, 1847.

SINCE my last, from China, of November 1st, I have had quite a chase on the lines of march between Monterey, Monte Morelas, and this place. About four thousand troops are thus far on the way towards Tampico. Taylor in command; but he has been ordered (by Scott, at Brazas) to return from here to Monterey, and remain in command on that line. The intention is, obviously, to move a large column from Vera Cruz to the capital, under Scott. Perhaps Taylor will move in that direction also, from Saltilla. From that, I presume that Scott and Taylor will so far interfere with each other's ideas of command, preference, &c., as to neutralize any feeling of opposition which either may have towards the Administration; and thus leave the President and Cabinet free to conduct this war as they think best.

An accident just occurred a few miles from our present camp, at a little town called Villa Grand. Lieutenant John Riches, bearer of despatches from Monterey to this column, was murdered by the townspeople, or "guerillas"—a kind of Light Horse Guards, organized by the States and towns for the protection of the settlements. These guerillas are not robbers, as some newspaper reporters assert; they are a species of Light Horse Cavalry, used extensively in this country for a century past, and, in fact, in all South America. But, under the name of guerillas, no doubt exists that many freebooters carry on their operations of robbery and depredation alike on friend and foe, under the guise of being guerillas.

Still, the guerilla proper is a time-honoured and well-defined troop, originating no doubt in times of harassment with the more savage heathens—in a climate where the Christians were little inclined to make pursuit on foot. Indeed, such heathens used horses, or ponies, and hence could be successfully pursued only on horseback. This led to a universal use of guerillas, or a kind of cavalry.

I closed my last on "antagonism" of our peoples with the close of the Revolution—a successful war, and, per consequence, a baker's dozen of "free colonies," so called. They had previously "set up shop" for themselves, under the firm of "Confederation," and a while after changed that firm, in its name and character, to "The United States," or "Union of States." I have expressed my utter want of confidence in the honesty of the motive which the colonies assigned for that rebellion. I have also expressed my abhorrence of the weakness, wickedness, and folly of a King and Parliament in the manner which they treated that rebellion. I feel sure that in no period of the history of the English Government and of the English people (both of whom I admire) have they ever shown so little statesmanship as was exhibited in their military efforts to hold on to an unwilling set of colonies. Had Chatham's voice, or Burke's appeal, been heeded, to "let them go: they will the sooner return if separation is wrong, or be as advantageous to England as to the colonies if separation is right." But such councils were not heeded, and hence followed the blood which makes the separation still to exist.

We now come to the formation of what was called a "more stable Government," the present Union, "the Constitution," and the legislation under it. I am going to consider this very briefly; only for the purpose of tracing the channels through which the antagonism I have mentioned becomes visible. In the very formation of that Constitution we plainly see the characteristics of the two classes I have specified, namely, the one favoring, even insisting on a strong Government—that is, a Constitution almost consolidating the States into one central Government. I need not tell you that the advocates of this were all commercial and manufacturing people—(there may have been here and there a convert to it of the other class; but, as a class, all agricultural people, that is, all the Southern States, and Middle States, opposed such concentration of power, and advocated only limited and specific powers to the Federal Government)—while the colonies (now called States) reserved all other powers to themselves. There was an actual conflict of ideas at the very outset touching the most vital nature of the Government to be formed; and we have, as the advocates of the two systems, the same classes we have divided the people into. But, what is stranger still, we find that class striving for a strong Government—to exercise constructive or implied powers—which had been the first to rebel against implied powers of the late Parliament! While, on the other hand, the agricultural class advocated the complete annihilation of all implied powers, and a specific code of expressed powers only. Query—does this not afford further evidence that the real motive of the one class was not so much to get rid of a strong Government, having implied powers over them, as it was merely to change the source of that power? I think it does. However, the conflict waxed warm, and continued long; and no reader of the debates in the several State Conventions can fail to see distinctly the real character of the Government which either class desired to form. But neither class was quite successful. A compromise was come to, and a Constitution was agreed upon (which we now have), limiting the Federal Powers to expressed objects, solely by dint of the agricultural efforts, and yet made as strong and as general, on the part of commerce and manufacturing classes, as they could. The result is called by most people very plain. I don't see it in such light. If all men and classes were honestly devoted to "peace and good-will among men," then the Constitution is perfect. But, with the "antagonism" I see in the two classes, it is a bone between Towser and Tray, and will yet have to be interpreted. Not because that instrument is wrong, but because it will stand in the way of "class interest" and coveted power ! Nothing is ever done without some kind of an excuse; so will the Constitution be made the excuse for—all things.

Already, under constructive powers, the commercial and manufacturing class demand the power more extensively to further its special trade—such as high tariffs, favoring home bottoms, fishing dues, &c., &c.,—and a part of the same class call for banks as fiscal agents, internal improvements, &c., &c.; while, pitted against this, as a class, is the whole agricultural districts, having against them of their own class only an isolated individual, now and then, whose life and study and associations have drawn him out of his natural family or class.

We here come to the plain path of conflict—physical and visible—between our two antagonistic classes. It is in the vocations of life which they have been driven to follow, not by accident, but by that pre-existing element of nature. It is not this vocation which causes the conflict; the vocation is only the avenue of bringing it on. The motive to conflict is "innate antagonism of two classes" which never should have formed a co-partnership. The means through which such conflict will be carried on are these diverse vocations and their cognates. The excuse for conflict will be the Constitution !

Hence we come to the final end of wise men's labours. Even their Constitution—their palladium, men's liberties —is what? Answer—it is the excuse to destroy them !

Affectionately,

PARMENAS.

LETTER IX.

Tampico, Mexico, January 30, 1847.

*   *   *   *   *   *

AFTER much hard marching and great harassment by rival generals, we arrived at this delectable place, and cleared off some hundred acres of thick underbrush to form an encampment. We are on the elevated banks of the Panuco River, which is an estuary or arm of the sea, coming up and extending round the city of Tampico, and extending far back into the interior. I understand we shall embark here for Vera Cruz in a few days or weeks. I wrote you from Victoria; but I half fear it will never reach you, because I sent it by the interior, or land express, to Matamoras.   Most of this army has marched from Monterey and Matamoras to this place, some 370 miles ; and I will state that I have never before known what it was to look at sugar, cotton, and rice lands. Nothing in the United States can even approximate to this climate and soil for sugar and rice; and for cotton, it is quite as good as any we have in Mississippi.

The nations of the Earth will not long suffer these heathen slothful people to occupy and not cultivate this vast region of country. Nations and people have their epochs, and Mexico has hers. Her religion, her morals, and her customs have been changed in the greatest haste, and with much violence. Her very traditions have been obliterated. All before the least diffusion of a general knowledge of Christianity and humanity has been extended to her people. The consequence is, her condition as a nation is gloomy in the extreme, and scarcely more so to the stranger than to her own subjects. They do not even evince a joy in the fruits of their own soil, for it is scarce theirs. Neither in the customs of their forefathers (the Aztecs), for they have just learned enough to despise their practices as debasing, yet not enough to lay hold of something higher. They have no interest in their laws, for they do not even originate in their behalf. They have lost their country. They cannot discover it to be their own nor their ancestors. So they live and move in what we might call a superstitious egotism. They cut loose from a Christian Government before they could go alone, and have, therefore, neither the intelligent patriotism of republican citizens, nor the loyalty of good subjects to a Crown. They hang midway between Christianity and heathenism with no force to start them either way. So much for liberty, referred to in my last, with no preparation in habits or manners to enjoy it!

My last letter closes our political dissertation on the visible physical elements of antagonism between the two classes of the American people. The peculiarities of this (Mexican) people offer striking proofs of my division, and of the characteristics of either. The same classes, too, exist here to some extent, though in the aggregate the whole people belong to the Southern or agricultural class. Still, even here (being a separate nation) the people are subdivided into the two classes, agricultural and mercantile, which combines the commercial and what little manufacturing they have. On my way down I had occasion to

purchase some iron to mend a wagon, and I paid the
usual market price, 31 cts. per pound, for it. Also I got
my horse shod at one dollar the shoe, being the usual
rates current. This will seem to indicate how extremely
puny are the manufacturing and mechanical interests here.
Notwithstanding, I will remark, for the especial benefit of
you people in the United States, that the duties on im-
ports in Mexico are about four times as high as in the
United States. Hence you will ask, why is this ? I will
answer. It is because the mercantile interest here controls the manufacturing also, and finds it easier to do such
work in foreign countries than here, because the mechanics
and other facilities are there ready at hand, while on the
other side, the people, the masses, are semi-heathen,
purely agricultural, and too ignorant and obtuse to understand their pecuniary interest or the means to secure
such. Hence the mercantile, i.e., commercial and manufacturing, has here got entire control of the creative or
agricultural. Hence excessive high duties depriving four-
fifths of the masses of all articles of comfort or refinement,
while the other fifth pay the enormous tariff on only a
portion which they otherwise would use. This commercial class then, though few in number, controls also
the productions of the soil, since they alone offer a market.
They regulate supply and demand, and the value of a
man's crop (be it sugar, cotton, rice, or maize) is just
what a few men may arrange amongst themselves to pay.
In other words, these few men fix the value of crops here
the same as Philadelphia or Wall Street brokers fix the
value of stocks or shares of certain railroads or other
corporations in the market. Just in this way, too, are
the mechanical and commercial interests in the Eastern
States trying to control the productions of the whole agricultural districts or States. They must and will control

them, or else fail in the attempt, which is not the history of such conflicts in the past.

I here find myself close to the subject which closed my last letter to you from Victoria, in which I remarked that the channels or avenues, through which the "inherent" antagonism of the two classes of people in the United States are to be manifested, are those appertaining to their special vocations. I, therefore, return to this subject. God has implanted in the hearts of all men many emotions in common. Many of their hopes and fears are common. Many of their tastes, desires, and passions are common; yet, as we have before said, there are some emotions of the human heart sufficiently diverse as to form the basis of our division into two classes. Then comes the intellectual endowment which still further demonstrates the existence of the inherent difference or antagonism. There are but two vocations or occupations for man on earth. You may subdivide the various pursuits of the human family as you will, yet there are but two classes, the one which lives by creating, the other which lives by that created. There is but one mode of creating. There are scores of changes and modifications to be wrought on that which is created. The world was scarce delivered over to man when these two modes of living or vocations were adopted by their respective votaries, i.e., the two classes referred to. These two vocations are called emphatically agricultural and mechanical. The talent or endowment "agricultural" is complete in itself, is passive, quiet, peaceful, deliberate, patient, and constant. Faith is the first element of its nature. It plants in faith. It cultivates in confidence. It reaps in the proud exultation of the enjoyment of the fruits of its faith. It is a slow process of acquiring what we call "worldly wealth;" yet it is this very slowness which adapts it to the natures of the class who follow it. It is the least cunning (we might say, the most obtuse), the least vigilant, because the least suspicious in its nature. It does not reason closely, because it deals in faith and not in reason. Being utterly without design on others, it suspects not others with designs on it. Now the mechanical is just the reverse in its nature. It is active, violent, and demonstrative. It has no faith, but deals only in certainty or proofs deduced from reason. It more and more learns to substitute reason for faith; its scepticism leads to inquiry. Inquiry brings out reason ; the faculty of reason thus becomes the test for all things. This is all very well, as far as reason is applicable; but finite minds cannot apply reason to all things ; and here, where it fails, the mechanical class drops the certain and stands on utter disbelief, while the other class, agricultural, goes on in faith to believe all things even unto super-stition. However, I have dwindled down into a more metaphysical dissertation than I had intended. I will return to the more practical view of the subject.

I have already remarked the early conflict of ideas in the National Congress as to the " powers conferred by the Constitution " to regulate and control the mechanical and commercial interests on the one side *versus* the agricultural on the other. This war or conflict of ideas still goes on, and while the apparent conflict may seem to be on subjects quite remote from a strife between the two opposite interests (agricultural and mechanical), yet such are only apparent, not real. The opposition lately to the admission of Texas into the Union on the part of some of the Northern (*i.e.*, manufacturing and commercial) States, was not because they desired no more States in the Union. Because, if the Union and Government of the United States is what it purports to be in theory, then it is as

well suited to a hundred States as to thirteen or twenty.
Neither was the large and respectable opposition in Texas
herself to going into that Union based on the theory of
that Union.

No. The Northern opposition was based on its
antagonism to agriculture, which was all the new State
possessed; while the opposition in Texas was based on a
distant cloud of mechanical and commercial pressure,
which is, and was then clearly visible on the horizon.
Neither party comes forward to assert its fears, because
the very presence of such fear would show want of confidence in the common chart, compact, or Constitution.
Still, such are the grounds of that opposition. There is
at this time a violent opposition in Congress to this war,
and a score of reasons are assigned for that opposition;
and no doubt the human heart has, in isolated cases, worked
itself up to the belief that the reasons are real; yet I assert
that no reality attaches to any one which the opposition
has yet assigned, while the real foundation of all objections
is in the deep, dark, hidden enmity of one class of pursuits
to another. Go back to 1820, when the State of Missouri
was suspended in the balance. Her admittance into the
Union was ostensibly opposed because she admitted negro
slavery; but it is folly to suppose such was the real ground
of objection.

No. It was because she came in with her whole
capital on the side of agriculture, *versus* the mechanical
and commercial. Let that State ever become commercial
and mechanical, and those who now oppose her would be
just as loth to part with her, slave or not slave. I cannot
refrain the remark just here, that the present opposition
in Congress to this war presents a most strange spectacle
of absurdity, because the whole cause of the war is on
account of commerce. Hence, the strongest champions

for its prosecution are the interested commercial men; while the balance of commercial men are opposing it, not because of its origin, in fact, but because of the results likely to be attained—to wit, a large addition to our domain, containing a purely agricultural people, whose representatives will advocate agricultural interests, *versus* mechanical and commercial. As I have before said, real causes of opposition are concealed, while false ones are substituted. Hence, as in the case of Missouri, some will aver that their opposition springs from a repugnance to slavery in Texas (and most likely to be in any State created south of that, or south of the parallel 33° 30′ from the Sabine). But this is not a real cause of opposition, because slavery already exists there, and has for three hundred years, and will till the heathen slave is Christianized, be it long or short. The opposition to Missouri, and the compromise line of slavery, was not because of slavery; it was because of the character of labour and productive capital which slaves gave to the States which had them. Those who oppose the extension of slavery in the North do it not because of slavery or the slave; they oppose its extension because it is well known that the heathen slave (be he Indian serf, Mexican peon, or African slave) always pursues entirely the agricultural vocation, and hence his owner represents the welfare, progress, and interest of agricultural pursuits, *versus* the commercial and mechanical. Neither does he who advocates the extension of slavery do so because he wants to continue to receive the slaves' labour *per se*. It is because he wants the benefits of agriculture, the slave by chance only being part of his means of obtaining it. You might as well say that the wealthy owner of an Eastern manufactory wants tariff benefits, because of his operatives, which we know is fallacious; he wants tariff to enable him to employ his capital in that work.

All these are the visible political antagonisms growing out of an inherent pre-existing antagonism bet.veen the two classes of people. And in this conflict all persons (of apparently intermediate status) will arrange themselves, according to circumstances, local interests, and lastly, natural bent.

More anon.

Affectionately yours,

PARMENAS.

LETTER X.

Vera Cruz, Mexico, April 15th, 1847.

*   *   *   *   *   *

MY long silence has been caused by the activity of mind and body in the military line of duty. We sailed from Tampico on the 26th of February; tarried awhile at Lobos Island, thence to Antonlizardo; landed at this place on the 9th of March; invested the city for a circuit of some sixteen miles; bombarded it till about the 27th, when it capitulated, and we now hold it. I was for eighteen days and nights on picket duty, without a change of clothes or water to wash my face; only raw pork and hard bread. We could make no fire to cook, because the smoke would make known our locality to the enemy; neither had I any bedding but my overcoat. In the mean-time we had a severe norther, which subjected me to extreme exposure: a dreadful cold and chill, which resulted in measles and mumps, so I am barely able to sit up to write. The army has mostly gone on to the interior *viâ* Cero Gorda. I shall try and visit New Orleans in a few days or weeks, as I feel utterly unable to do duty. My regiment remains here to garrison this place, which is

not hopeful for field duty; I cannot, therefore, go on to
the interior, to the high atmosphere of the table-lands or
mountains.   I hope you will be able to meet me in New
Orleans : write me there to St. Charles' Hotel, and say
what time I may expect you.   You will have learned all
the particulars of the military movements from the newspaper correspondents.

Affectionately yours,

PARMENAS.

LETTER XI.

Convent, St. Domingo, Mexico, March 5th, 1848.

*   *   *   *   *   *

I HAVE just closed a long march from Vera Cruz to this
place, forming part of an escort to the largest wagon-train
of supplies that I have ever seen on the road at any one
time.   My health is very far from satisfactory—in fact,
unless I improve I must seek quiet and release from all
duty.   I have volunteered for an expedition across the
mountains (in the direction of Accapulco), where the
climate is said to be fine.   I will leave some time during
this month, and may not find it convenient to write you
soon again.

What a theme for study this country and people furnish to the philosophical mind ! The country itself having
every variety of climate, soil, and production, containing
untold mineral resources, and a variety and grandeur of
scenery beyond description; but the people attract my
attention more than the country, though they evidently
belong to each other in many respects.   It is now almost
a year since I "bored" you with my views on "classes"

in the United States, but I have not failed to jot down a
few ideas on that subject, induced to some extent by the
character presented to my mind here of the people. In a
previous letter somewhere I remarked that I had passed
out of a " preacher-ridden" Government into a " priest-
ridden " one. The " Convent St. Domingo," therefore, in
which I am quartered, may be a fit place to give my views
on this matter of " preachers " and " priests," for there is
a vast difference in the parts they perform. I hope you
will not consider me irreverent, nor yet personal, when I
express my want of regard for either class, as I find them
in life; the fact is, I am not a little disposed to lay the
foundation of my two classes in this matter of so-called
religion. I have already said that the manifestations of
antagonism, or the means of its developing or showing
itself, are in the worldly products, or the gains, or the
remunerations, if you please, of two kinds of vocations;
but the " antagonism" itself is deeper and anterior.
Now, it occurs to me that man's vocation is mainly, if not
entirely, induced by reason of his ideas of existence after
death; furthermore, no nation or people on earth that
we know of, or have ever known, failed to shape their
customs, habits, manners, and social relations, entirely by
their ideas of service to a Creator : hence, I think it is
obvious that this religious belief must be one of the
elements of extreme antagonism. Certainly, more blood
has been shed on account of religion than for any other
cause. Even where those of the same creed were pitted
against each other, one cannot tell but what their common
confession is one of tradition, or of forced compliance,
rather than an intelligent conviction in like faith. We
certainly look in vain for any people whose temporal
government is not really founded on their religion, so that
the cause of trouble and dissension is always a religious

E

rather than a political one. The "Catholic Church" was not called so very long—it was soon the "Roman Catholic Church," the "Roman" being the whole civil polity of the State; and it soon dragged down the ecclesiastical to the level of temporal Government. Our own Government is an attempt to keep the ecclesiastical and civil distinct, but, so far from being successful, I think it is permitting the religious to absorb almost entirely the political, by the very disconnection specified in the Constitution; that is to say, I think it is fast becoming a politico-religious Government instead of a political one. In Mexico the *de facto* Government is the "Church," while its adjunct, or aid, is the nominal political organisation. In the United States the *de facto* Government is at present political, with the religious spirit supplying its whole life and motion. In Mexico political measures are such only when they are sanctioned by the Church. In the United States political measures are potent and popular only when they come charged with the religious zeal and sectarianism of a dominant Democracy. In Mexico, statesmen are only supplied from the "Church," or by its authority, and represent ecclesiastical instead of political ideas. In the United States statesmen are passing away, and their places are filled by politicians who embody and represent a religious league instead of a political organisation. The exclusive character of the Church in Mexico binds the individual intellect to a blind confession of its dogmas, and supplies mental culture only in that mode which warps the intellect, stifles scepticism, and therefore prevents inquiry. In the United States the complete independence of Church and State in theory gives unlicensed scope to each organisation to pursue its inquiry, irrespective and theoretically regardless of the other, while, in both countries man's every action being governed mysteriously by his unwritten inexplicable faith, his legislation will always show signs of a religious bias: hence, while the United States is in theory a civil Government, yet, on this very account it is compelled to admit in practice whatever of religious enthusiasm its Democracy may possess; so that, in course of time, when the various sects or creeds have run their course (as they most certainly will ere long), you will find them "pairing off," like joining like, so that only two classes will then be formed; and, at that period will be concentrated the elements of antagonism perfect for a conflict. No such inherent antagonism exists in Mexico, because, all being of one religion, there is nothing to encounter. Now, as it is impossible to form a civil Government separate from the religious elements of the people, in its practical workings, it appears to me that there is a judicious safety in a well-devised connection of the two by statute, rather than a broad ignoring of the whole evil by theory, where a practical interference was and is unavoidable. This restrains the religious from extravagant interference, and secures time to the political to effect a change. The evils of this Church Government in Mexico do not result from the political, but from the Church polity; neither do the evils come from the Church *per se*, but from the polity it has thought necessary for defence against future political combinations which are only feared. The nation cannot exist, nor the people abide, without "the Church," or some religion; this religion cannot exist without shaping their habits, manners, and customs; but their habits and manners do form their political status, which must either conform to, or run counter to, any other political system which has been set up. Here, then, is an unavoidable point of conflict but you will say the United States escapes this because she has no connection between the political and the

ecclesiastical, or religious: this I deny. Her political
theory, I know, admits of no connection; but, the moment
that theory is to be put into practice, then it is entirely
governed by the habits, manners, and customs of her
people; but their habits and customs are the result of the
people's religious theories and practices. Now, if all
religious theories and practices were unchangeable—if
they remained the same yesterday, to-day, and for ever—
then I admit that the civil or political code could very
well be so framed and adjusted as to avoid collision; but
such is not the character of religious liberty anywhere:
if it were, it would cease to be religious liberty, since it
would then be as here, in Mexico, confined to fixed
dogmas. We therefore come to the unavoidable conclu
sion that either your political system must be left open for
constant change and modification, so as to conform to the
constant daily and annual fluctuations in religious sentiment, or else you must make the religious stationary.
The latter is the condition in Mexico, where, to make it
doubly sure of stability, "the Church" holds all the keys
of education, moral culture, and physical habits. This
insures a political system in harmony with the religious.
The reverse is the case in the United States: there the
political is fixed, which does not form the habits, manners,
and customs, but which is formed by the habits; while the
religious, which does form those habits, is left unbridled
scope within the range of all man's passions, prejudices,
tastes, and inclinations. But you will say that I am
wrong—that the political is not fixed, but changes at will
by the very people. So they do in localities, and to too
great an extent in States; but I assert that the Federal
Constitution is fixed, in comparison with the rapid change
around it, outside of it, and over it. It is susceptible of
change and modification, it is true; but not with sufficient

ease and frequency as to be able to keep out of the way of religious interference, or of the rapidly-changing habits and manners of the people. You will say, then, make it of easier modification: then your Federal system will be unstable, because too certain of constant change. Now, I fear that in all I have said I may be misunderstood, and that you will at once jump to the false conclusion that I am making too close acquaintance with " the Church," or Roman Catholicism. Such is not the fact. I have been comparing two opposite extremes, without condemning or adopting either. I will say more—I have no kind of affiliation with the system here : the Mexican people are as yet only in the early dawn of enlightenment, and still possessing a superstitious bigotry. The Church, which is the fountain of all instruction, the source of all power, and of every rule of action, both moral and physical, is a carcase, with all inside of it decayed, except a series of formulas and traditions, equally with the corpse, devoid of one element of life or of vitality. Their religion is one of the body, not of the heart; it is entirely of physical exercise, not of a heart-felt intellectuality; it is solely and entirely a service of bodily exercise, rotating about certain fixed axes, confining it within certain fixed limits—in other words, feeding solely on the word which " killeth," and excluding the spiritual, which is " life." The legitimate object of religion (which is spiritual life) is entirely lost sight of in the purely worldly acquisitions which its systematic formulas secure to the higher officials who administer them. The sanctification and acceptance of the priest is at once the sufficient atonement for his own sins and those of his people. God may accept the people because the heathen, who hath not the law, are a law unto themselves; but the priest must be judged by the law. On the other hand, the United States presents the opposite extreme. Religion there is purely intellectual; it has neither formulas nor traditions about which to rotate; it flounders about in space, jostling its neighbour, colliding at times, and even falling to atoms, but is soon repaired by metaphysical cement, and a few timbers of rationalism. The religion there excludes all physical action, and is only an exercise of reason. What is not reasonable is false, what cannot be proved by a regular course of logic is thrown out: hence, in Mexico, the senseless motions of visible exercise are supposed to produce unseen and mysterious results; while in the United States religion is the unseen exercise of one's reason, without regard to manner or motion, and from the full and proper exercise of which all physical relations will be shaped and modified. This is the superstition of ignorance; that the superstition of reason. In Mexico all reason is extinct, or else prostituted to the infallibility of faith. In the United States all faith is subject to the test of reason. Here belief alone exists, because faith is the only soil necessary for its growth. In the United States temporal knowledge alone exists, because it is the only fruit which reason alone will produce. In Mexico the priest is estimated solely by his theology, his dogmas, and his formulas. In the United States the preacher is estimated solely by his character, his actions, and his reason. Religious controversies are daily going on in the United States which would incur the instant anathemas of "the Church" in Mexico (only distant three days post). Meanwhile the political habits of localities in the United States keep even pace with and conform to the march of the religious. Query—Can a written Constitution (unless speedily and frequently modified) stand the test of "Reason," unaccompanied by those other elements of Faith and Charity? I think not. Reason does not admit of either Faith or Charity. Neither has Reason any hope; because it already hath the certainty demonstrated, and hence has no room for the useless element—"Hope." But I am getting into the field of "Fraternity," which, in the United States Government, occupies the place which Charity does in the Government of God. If a people foster Reason to the exclusion of Faith, then will their habits and manners be shaped accordingly. But if Reason excludes Charity, then must Fraternity also be on the decline. Ultimately it will be extinct. Then what? Why, nothing very extraordinary —only what you see in England, France, Russia, Prussia, Austria, &c. That is a Government in which Church and State will be connected, and will be either a despotism or a monarchy. But I think it is a big jump from an "Universalism" to an "Absolutism," and a "Constitutional Union of States" will have but a poor chance to escape the gulf between, which is a conflict in blood. Fraternity, the only legal weapon, destroyed, then will come Reason for and against. Faith, Hope, Charity, will then be unknown. Fraternity in the United States Government will then be as dead as is the spiritual in Mexico. Both nations are on the road to ruin, but in opposite directions and from opposite causes!

Affectionately yours,

PARMENAS.

LETTER XII.

Cuernavaca, Mexico, May 15, 1848.

*   *   *   *   *   *

In my last, from the capital of Mexico, I referred to the opposite extremes of the religious tendencies in Mexico compared with those in the United States. That both nations are tending rapidly to great dangers, though in opposite directions. That the Church or religion of Mexico governs almost entirely the State, and, being at a complete standstill, little or no progress is made in any thing useful in her political system. But while the Church has and does shape her political course almost entirely, yet there are points in which the Church fails to command entire control. And in this single respect is the political now beginning to move (barely perceptible) distinct from the Church rule. As I have before said, this Government adopted nearly entire our own Constitution of a Federal character, yet the character and the habits of the people of the United States which made that Constitution efficient for them to the present time, was utterly wanting in the Mexican people, and hence made the same form of Government mere mockery with them. Still its adoption, though at first weak, and of apparently no effect for a few years, has created a bare semblance of political action in a few minds which, I doubt not, may one day feel competent to even challenge the authority of the Church in the civil government here. But it will be some time first, and may count on many defeats. The result, both in its time and effect, will depend very much on the influence which this war, and the associations with our army, may have on the minds of the masses with whom we have come in contact.

I lived several weeks in the house of President Peñy-y-Peñy. He fully understands the nature of our system of Government, but he also sees the utter impossibility of inaugurating the same among the Mexicans at the present time. It would require the immediate separation of Church and State, which event would necessitate the disposing of the immense landed interests or domains now held by and belonging to the Church, by which means alone can the large revenues be directed from the ecclesiastical to the political authority. The Church revenues for only a few years would suffice to pay even the National Debt. But the Church will never willingly consent to any such use of her benefits for various reasons; but a sufficient one is, that such payment would give impetus to a power and influence antagonistic to her own. Still, the entering wedge of inquiry has been inserted, and may or may not be gradually driven through the dull mass of intellect; and when so driven may or may not find political acumen or moral honesty enough to produce fruits. Two grand parties are wanted here at present, both to be governed by principle; one for, the other against, the present union of Church and State. Minor parties there are already enough to destroy the country; but two great parties on opposite principles would very soon culminate into a healthy conflict of two opposite systems, both based on a principle, and therefore commanding the hearty and honest advocacy of high moral worth and talent. Until this occurs, however, little can be expected from any change in Mexican Government. The present numerous parties or cliques only harass and disturb the whole body politic without any results except the wasting of energy and corrupting the political morals and integrity of the people.

Query. Are not the United States in the same category at this present time, divided into miserable small parties, neither able to effect anything in general legislation,—in fact having nothing real to effect except a gradual undermining of political honesty and endeavouring to instil a poisoned kind of patriotism for the real? In one of your letters some years since, you expressed great joy at what you considered the rapid passing away of the two great parties, Federal and Republican, because you at once concluded that the numerous smaller cliques or parties which were taking their places would neutralise each other, and thus remove even the shadow of danger to our system of Government. Now, I think if you will examine more closely the moral effects of these local and sectional parties or cliques, you will find they are and have been sowing the only seeds of real danger. These smaller parties are the very agents at work to cultivate the seeds of the antagonism I have asserted to exist. This antagonism, though existing in a latent state, would never become manifest, and hence do no harm just as long as two great parties only existed, both acting from moral principles of honest conviction; but the moment these great parties subside, then general quiet ensues, and in this quietude does the element of inherent antagonism find time and opportunity to insinuate itself, select its defenders, and work out its lines or avenues of progress. It has nothing to do with principles; it deals solely in expediencies and self or sectional interests. Hence it never commands the attention of great minds till it has well nigh encased itself in an impenetrable network of local prejudices and interests.

By this period of its progress, however, it has corrupted the masses, and all principles are then lost sight of in self-interest, or, as in the United States, in geographical products. Now this appears to me to be just now going on as rapidly in the United States as it is here; the only difference being in the fact that the American people have a greater distance to travel, more people to corrupt and render obtuse to moral principle, a larger amount of intelligence to overcome, and a breastwork of moral honesty to encounter before they consummate the end.

The Mexicans, on the contrary, have but short distances to travel, and have no fixed habits of a just Government to overcome, little intelligence, and less moral honesty.

Hence they have got to the abyss of anarchy, misrule, and violence. Already the American parties are going apace, and the period at which they will arrive at the same condition will be measured by the difference in velocity between their religious zeal and rationalism and the slower motion of our constitutional application of fixed political principles, the intensity of the same being equally increased. The very rapid advance in change, of social habits, customs, and manners in the United States, caused mainly by an unbridled religious frenzy, and the application of reason to everything (or, to bring it down to what it is, and is determined to be), a levelling dominant democracy must stop, or the Constitution must permit radical political changes, or else a conflict must ensue. One of these three effects will certainly be produced.

This spirit of democracy is not equally prevalent, however, in all parts of the United States, and hence the more certainly will it create disruption. (Now I do not wish you to misunderstand me when I thus speak of "Democracy," for you are so sensitive on the subject that I am in constant danger of being misconstrued). I know you belong to the so-called Democratic party, as understood in the South; but I have already called your attention to the fact, that such is not the same Democratic party of the North. That of the South I have called Republican, which, of course, is also Democratic when comparing the whole United States Government with a monarchy or an absolute government, but which, in comparing the North with the South, the latter is not so Democratic as the North. This is evident from the character, nature, and habits of the two classes of people who settled the two sections of country. The Northern or New England people were a religious democracy when they first landed on these shores. It was the " religious democracy" of those people which induced the English Government to be rid of them. And it is from the same element of democracy that the emigrants from England, Germany, Scotland, and France that have been increasing the population of the Northern States for ninety years. The Northern States are all subjected to these influences, and in consequence of them, are becoming intensely democratic; while the small parties into which they are divided for no general principles, but only political preferment, have each their violent partizan leaders engaged in corrupting the masses as rapidly as possible by constant agitation and elections. This religious, democratic frenzy has full, absolute sway; and since the disappearance of your two great national parties, nothing has existed to counteract or neutralise the evil tendencies.

I do not say the same evils of a similar kind have, or do now exist in the Southern States. To some extent they may, but are scarcely perceptible. But other changes are going on with you, which, in effect, will be the counterpart of the change in the North. The South is too slow in religious socialisms—the North too fast; and while both are progressing, and that not slowly, yet the North so much the faster that the South seems to stand still.

This would be no ground for apprehension were it not for the fact that the rapidly moving North is becoming so Democratic, or if the South were making timely changes in the Constitution to meet the inevitable changes in manners, customs, and religions of the North people. It is the beauty of the English Government which secures this equilibrium. But the South is neither adjusting her constitutional relations with the Federal system, nor is she progressing in any change of religious habits or customs to enable her to acquiesce in the pressure from the North. But you remark, in one of your letters, that "the Constitution is the guide" to all parties. Now, I admit it was the guide, and, to some extent, is so yet; but, as I have time and again said, good as it was, and good as it is, yet they are merely relative terms. Whatever our Constitution is, it was the product of certain manners and habits and religious tendencies of a people. So are all Constitutions. Now, if you let the Constitution alone for a period long enough, the habits, manners, and religion of that same people will have so completely changed that they will not recognise their own work. It will have become the lifeless work of a deceased people.

I know you think differently. You hold to the idea that, while the law stands, it will be enforced by common consent; and perhaps you so think from experience. So it would in England or in Russia, but not so in a "Democracy." Your life as well as mine are too short, as is that of any one man to judge of these matters by his own field of observation. In this matter of compacts or Constitution for a Confederacy or common Government, we must take history. We thus learn that all nations make inroads in their laws, while Democracies are perfectly rampant to ride over and defy, at times, the written code. I fear the United States will not be an exception. Monarchical or absolute Governments make fewer and slower changes than Republics. This is inevitable: it is either a curse or a blessing of Democracy to change rapidly and often,—the world has not yet decided which. Absolute Governments agree that it is a great curse. Democracies themselves say it is the acme of perfection in liberal, free government. With the greatest filial regard, and with perfect respect for my father's Democracy and views, I am constrained to say I view Democracies as unbridled tyrants, with power and will to do anything that the concentrated wickedness of the populace may see fit. The Northern States is such a Democracy, or is fast becoming such. The South is not, and never will be such, because the natures of the people are different; they have no manners, no customs, no habits tending to it, nor did they ever have such tendencies. Hence they are, so to speak, a different nation from the North: and the continued effect of a dominant Democracy to force a similarity where God has made an incrasable line of distinction thousands of years ago, will result in like conflicts, which have always occurred between the same classes all over the world.

A thousand supposed (but false) reasons will then be assigned as the cause of such conflict. So it always is. A few taxes by Parliament was assigned as the cause of the Colonial revolt against England. So millions yet believe. I am not one of them. I feel no doubt but the true cause was religious antagonism; and, hence, would not have received the co-operation of the Catholic and Church States if all motives and the secret of heart could have been known.

Affectionately yours,

PARMENAS.

LETTER XIII.

Hacienda, Trinidad, May 30th, 1848.

I HAVE been ordered over into this region to protect the proprietors of some large haciendas (or plantations) from violence by the revolt of their "peons," or serfs. I am on the slope, bearing west towards Acapulca, some forty miles from Cuernabaca. I have had considerable intercourse with these large haciendas and their mode of management. The owners, or proprietors, are most refined gentlemen, and possessed of all the gallantry and chivalrous hospitality so well known to belong to the Spanish gentleman. On these large estates—where sugar, cotton, coffee, &c., are grown—it is not unusual to find from three hundred to eight hundred peons, or serfs. Perhaps I had best call them serfs, as they differ somewhat from our slaves in the United States. Hence you will want to know just what a peon is. I shall, therefore, explain what it is; but, in so doing, I shall take occasion to hit your "democratic-free-labour-competition" system a lick which I think it justly deserves.

In the first place, slavery once existed in this country, and would yet, I presume, if that noble race (the Spaniard) who conquered it had kept it. But I have already lamented the separation from a Christian nation of this Mexican people at too early a period to make anything of themselves; so I will not recur to that again, any further than to exhibit still more of its evils. The evils I then mentioned were mostly of a religious or spiritual kind. I will here refer to the evils of a political kind. I have before said somewhere in my letters that freedom is imaginary. The whole world hath proved that. God hath said so; and Christ saith, neither the freeman nor the bondman is anything. But living, eating, drinking, and sleeping, are not imaginary : these are real, actual, and tax the energies (mental and physical) of three out of four of all free people. Slaves are not so much exercised about their eating, nor clothing. When slavery was abolished here, there was a large majority of the people who were utterly incapable of self-preservation. Five out of six of them fell victims to poverty and crime in the great scuffle which free competition of labour brought about. They had either to steal or beg. This was followed by a system of contracting debts with the principal proprietors of estates, which they could not pay. Failing to pay soon put a stop to further credit. Then began theft. To remedy this, the Government passed laws enabling the proprietors, or creditors, to hold the person or persons for the debt, at so much per week or month for his labour. This, then, was at once the establishment of the "social system," called "villienage," or serfage. The person who thus became the vassal, or peon, to a gentleman for a debt of ten dollars, at once made his domicile on his premises, and formed part of the household and estate; so did his family if he had any. His weekly allowance in pay, so far from paying his debt, did not even suffice to pay for his feed and clothing—still less for that of his family—with all which he was, and is, regularly charged in account-books kept for the purpose. Hence, in one year, if not less, he found himself tenfold deeper in debt than at first; and then his family, male and female, were all passed over under the laws, as peons also. This is peonage, or serfage; and it is not unusual to find five hundred peons on a plantation of this kind. These peons are sold, also, from one Duaña to another; but common consent keeps families together. You will thus perceive that the peon is a slave, yet without the advantages of the African slave, or that of the "villien" of former periods; because he is not cared for in sickness and old age, as those are, but can only claim such to the extent of his weekly earnings; or, if he receives more (as he does), it is a gratuity not obligatory on the owner. This is one step towards an improvement, however, over the destitution now, and for years, extant in all Europe on account of "liberty," in the midst of competition of labour. The world is getting rabid for freedom—freedom of labour. I have been over a large portion of the world, and from what I have seen the effects of competition of labour are most cruel and damning! It is starving millions who were once happy and well fed and clothed. France, England, Austria, Prussia, and Poland, and Hungary, are suffering this day countless miseries by this "freedom to starve if you can't get work." It is filling prisons, debasing women, and drying up the fountains of parental and filial affection! The monasteries and peonage here relieve this to some extent, but in a miserably unjust mode, since it limits the responsibility of the owner to the serf's nominal wages! But the evils of "competing labour" are in their infancy in Mexico, because none of those great improvements in labour-saving machinery have yet appeared. Hence, all can come more nearly finding work. But not so in the European countries I have named. In the United States (in the North) the evils of competing labour are already beginning to be felt, and but for the great outlet in the West it would be unbearable in a few years longer. As it now is, however, it is severely felt; and will demand an outlet in the Slave States. It will demand this as a temporary relief, and as a subterfuge to cover its total failure in supporting the great labouring mass of man. Socialism throughout France and England, and now beginning in the North-eastern States, is nothing else than an attempt to remedy a great evil brought about by free competing labour, which began at the discontinuance of serfage!

You know nothing of pauperism. No such thing exists in a slave country. In a slave country, or a serfage community, there exists the only kind of socialism which is worthy of the name. Such is, in fact, a community where each one loves his neighbour. Hence, in slave or serf countries you seldom find all the thousand and one societies purporting to be for the relief of the needy, because there are none. The owners see to this—not by the dollar, or by the visit, but freely and purely—because it is his.

Now, you will count me very strange to talk thus about liberty—the cradle in which I was rocked, and the shanty in which I was raised! Well; let us see. What is liberty here on earth? It is not to do as you please, for the laws restrain you on every hand. It is not to seek happiness in your own way, for in this you are restricted. There is no definition for liberty that I know of, except what the political economist gives us, which amounts to this—that a man is at liberty to compete with his neighbours and all others in the world for his food and raiment. This looks like a vast privilege; but let us see. Four out of five of the human family are incapable of competition. They are either too slow, too indolent, too weak, or too simple; but the fifth one is astute, active, cautious, dishonest, or in some other way takes the prize. He monopolizes the substance of four; and at once puts the four to bidding against each other for the labour which it only requires two or less to perform. He who gets it fares well; he who fails must starve! This is the true effect of free-competing-labour throughout the world; and I would be false to my duty and heartfelt conviction if I did not go further, and say it is the direct effect of Jefferson's false and infidel expressions in the very beginning of the Declaration of Rights; viz., that all men are equal, &c. I have before made allusion to the falsity of his theory; and the whole universe, not only unequal and enslaved man, but the whole animal and vegetable kingdom, prove it false! Men are unequal, not free; not at liberty to pursue happiness in their own way; because I helped to hang several for having pursued their line of happiness in their own way by depredating on others.

Philosophers and political economists ought to be

chained together, and fed on bread and water; and led round over the country (in which they affect to offer rules for), and let see something of practical life and of human nature; for of all men, I think they are the most narrow-minded and short-sighted. Now, you will at once class me anti-democratic, because of my views about liberty. I will take occasion ere long to show more fully the absurdity of the talk of the liberty philosophers and political economists, and of nearly all our politicians; while I shall maintain that your democracy affects it not, nor is it affected by it.

Affectionately,

PARMENAS.

LETTER XIV.

Austin, Texas, Dec. 30th, 1848.

I HAD the pleasure to receive your long letter of 30th September last, but have been too much engaged to find time to answer it until now. This is no detriment, however, because I have improved the time to read the more carefully what you have said; and I design, now, to answer some of your objections to my previously expressed views. You fall back, as usual, on the terms of our Constitution; yet, I have never objected to one word of that instrument. I fully acknowledge it to be all you say it is in word and letter; you assert, however, that the Constitution alone is sufficient to secure perfect peace and harmonious Government between all the States. I say it is not. This is a simple difference of opinion; secondly, you say that mutual interest between the Confederate States is also sufficient to secure the same end, and that both these forces are "ample for any emergency." I think you are mistaken

F 2

in both ; first, the Constitution is specific in its powers
and limitations, as you say; are not all Constitutions the
same? All Democracies we know of, as also all Republics,
had written Constitutions, or the equivalent; and all
specific, so far as it was designed they should have action,
yet they failed to secure what they were designed to secure.
Ours will fail in like manner, because a Constitution is
only the product of certain habits and customs prevalent
among the people who originate it, and agree to make it
the rule of action in certain cases; hence, a Constitution
of some kind is not a mere accident; it is a necessary
consequence of certain habits of life; but our written
Constitution is the same to-day as it was half a century
ago, or nearly so, while the habits of three-fourths of the
people have changed amazingly. You say that instrument can be changed; so it can, but only in a certain
way. That way has not yet been tried, and could not be
tried to-day, because of the very extreme dissimilarity
between the very people whom it was made to govern.
They were more nearly alike when they first made it;
now they are widely different; in fact, they were not half
so similar when they agreed to it, as they imagined; they
only appeared to each other in a true light when they
came to be compared by that one common standard, while
they have gone on separating more and more ever since.
Constitutions, strictly so, govern only stable representative
communities; the whole United States is not such a
community. The Southern States are comparatively stable
and representative; the Northern States are not. These
latter are Democracies already, and will be excessively so
in a short time. Not only do their citizens, by natural
increase, advance rapidly on into a Democratic mass, but
those States receive nine-tenths of the emigrants from
the old countries, and all of such emigrants are Radical

Democrats; they are the very pestiferous, revolutionary characters, which European nations are more than happy to get rid of. The man who fails to look at this, fails to see the imminent dangers awaiting the North. But the South is connected with the North by this same Constitution. The Northern Democracy will one day roll up that instrument as a scroll and waste paper. They cannot avoid it; it is their destiny (when unrestrained by stable laws). The *vox populi* is their Constitution. You count on men who will be constitutional observers in the North, but you count on what you will fail to find. How can one man resist a hundred? Now, I don't say this evil will come in a year, nor in ten years. I can't tell how rapidly this spirit of "Democratic equality" will progress in the North. It may come sooner or later. Come it will, unless something checks that progress. The Constitution is a safe guarantee, so long as it is the rule of action. But it ceases to be such just when you most need it. Hence, I will say, that if the Constitution saves the country, then will I have proved the existence of a Government without any written Constitution, because in a pure Democracy that which we have is as none. You seem to give your Constitution a kind of materiality; because you can see a piece of paper, you seem to clothe it with some of the powers of material resistance, as if it were a mountain, or an impassable river or lake. It is not so; it is all imaginary. The Constitution is nothing. The observance of what is recorded makes up all there is of it; but, as I have said, observance of it is absolutely impossible; *vox populi* of a wild Democracy takes its place. I repeat, that its observance by a "Democracy" is utterly impossible, because such Democracy never suffers any restraints, whereas your Constitution is made up of restraints. So much for the Constitutional guarantee!

Now, as it regards your "bond of mutual interests." You say the North needs the South and West to supply her with food, raw material, and to occupy her ships, &c. This would seem to be true, and, in fact, is true to that extent. But Democracy is not content with but half a loaf! She clamours for the other half! She wants higher tariffs. She despises that agriculture which objects to high duties. The North wants nothing but high tariffs. This is all she now begs for. She has kept her paid agents in Congress for fifty years to secure this; but the South has objected to this. The South must submit, or else this "dominant Democracy" will force them. It is only a matter of time. The West is in pretty much the same fix as the South; but the manufacturing States can manage them better, because the East are pushing out to the West their own men and money, and favouring, by every means, the immigration thither of those red-republican or solid democratic elements from Germany, France, England, Ireland, Hungary, and Austria. The South don't favour this class, because she is not a Democracy. These elements will be ten times more merciless and unconstitutional in their demands, as well as in their mode of legislation, than the native Americans have been. In fact, these are the tools which will do the voting, and the legislating will be done by the partisan leaders. Besides, the high tariffs affect the North-western agriculturalists less than the Southern people, because much of the products of North-west go South for bread, and hence never pass through the tariff exchange-avenues; and also, the West is advancing with considerable manufacture, which retains among them no small amount of the proceeds of those tariffs. All these things are beyond the reach of the South. The South has but one remedy in warding off conflict in this matter of "mutual interest" you speak of, which is to acquiesce in any amount of tariffs which manufactures and commerce choose to impose, and substitute her own manufactures in defence. This is the line of antagonism in this country and in our Government.

The South had best not employ herself with long, logical, and constitutional speeches in Congress as to their rights in the use and protection of slavery; because the North do not object to slavery, *per se*. What they object to is the power of the agricultural people; the North don't care a farthing what kind of labour is used in agriculture. It is enough for them to restrict its influence, whether it be black or white—free or bond. It is true that the North makes loud lamentations over negro slavery; and they pretend to put it on philanthropic grounds, but this is only to secure the co-operation of that class of European emigrants among them whose votes they rely on to control their elections, and whose excessive zeal for freedom (like a man suddenly in possesion of riches he knows not what to do with) makes them good tools to work with. It is not because they care anything about negro slavery *per se*. It is possible they think that negro slavery secures more unity of action in the agricultural States on political matters than any other kind of labour would admit of, and hence this would be another good political reason for wishing to diminish the present negro slavery in the South; but this is all. Their philanthropy in opposition to slaves is just the same as lies at the bottom of my philanthropy in opposing my neighbour's riches—because I have not an equal amount. This is its length, and depth, and breadth! I am intimately acquainted with many leading abolitionists in the North, and I have often heard them say, that the negro was "just where he ought to be, and he would be of no use except as a bondsman, and that all they wished to do by the agitation of the question was to weaken the power of the agricultural States in the national Congress so as to legislate more for the interest of manufacturers and the commercial marts." Knowing these facts, I say that the South should not be defending a false attack on the part of the violent partisans of "Northern Democracy."

You must, therefore, see that this "band of mutual interest" is not going to suffice long to secure the kindly feelings of the two "classes," because it hath already almost ceased to be of mutual interest. If the South could induce a large emigrant population of "Radical Democracy" to settle among them, then would she also take up the march of rapid Democracy; but even in such case they would be antagonistic to the Eastern people. But this she will not do, because her "class" of people are averse to it; and you, with all your so-called "Democracy," would be the first to shrink from the rabid, wild, unmeaning, and senseless vaporings of such a mass as I have seen in Northern cities.

The fact is, father, you must take a quiet trip out West, and up to the Lakes, thence on East, and observe a little of the working of that Democracy before you become its blind defender.

You will find a physical prosperity that will astonish your senses. A development most extraordinary, and deserving of all praise, admiration, and imitation, save and except in its utter prostitution of virtue, integrity, and political morals. All these elements of durability are rapidly declining—will soon become extinct in their growing Democracies. Then we shall see what the rapid advance in worldly development, in populations, and improvements, &c., are worth. For this we must wait.

Affectionately yours,

PARMENAS.

LETTER XV.

This letter was written by George Turnley, Esq., of Jefferson County, Tennessee, to his Grandson (the Author of the preceding letters in this book).

Dandridge, Tennessee, July 4, 1847.

My mind has entertained the subject of writing to you for a while past, and this desire is in no wise diminished since I have read some letters from you to your father And while it is not my expectation to finish a letter to-day, yet, it being our "Independence Anniversary," it fully entered my mind to begin one, and I shall continue it from time to time as the working of the spirit within me and my poor old feeble hand shall permit. This day calls to mind, afresh, the time when our great and wise men dictated and published to the world our Declaration of Rights under Civil Government, and, in the efforts to establish which I did what was in my power to effect. My father, long since gone—whence I, too, must soon follow—and who lies buried not far from where I write this, differed with me at that time to some extent; not that he felt any objections to the Declaration of Rights, then announced by the thirteen colonies, but because he felt that most of the Rights claimed could and would be secured ultimately from our mother-country without a Revolution; and also he was resting under the obligations which his oath imposed (taken the day he sailed from Liverpool for the New World), which was, that he would "never take up arms against his King and Parliament." However, he, like many others, had to acquiesce in the powers then present around him, and we made our Declaration good by more than six years of hard war, and we made our own Government, which is called, and is in fact, a free Government in contra-distinction to a monarchical Government: that is, we made a Republican Government

—in the which the "sovereign power" rests with the people, and is delegated from time to time to Representatives chosen by those who are to be governed. Therefore it is we say, with some truth, "that we govern ourselves" by choosing for our agents a President, Vice-President, and Members of a House of Commons, or Congress, and also we choose, through the State Assembly, our Senators. Hence, you see the people actually choose the agents who are to make the laws, and a President who is to see that the same are executed. All this really seems very plain and simple, and was so considered in the beginning. It certainly is very simple if properly studied and practised. But in after years it does appear to have become somewhat complex. This complexity, too (and which appears to be increasing), I fear, sometimes is going to be a great stumbling-block in the path of peace and good-will; and while I have an abiding faith in the agents of our Government chosen by the individual voice of every intelligent free man, yet it does appear to me that there is too much disposition to extend, and make too common this liberty to vote, and also too much tendency to multiply laws, all over the country, and, as it were, to supply a profession for a class of idle folks called lawyers.

But I am now tired of this present writing, and will defer further remarks till another day. I am getting well on to one hundred years of age, and can do many things better than write, especially ride my old favourite horse, which I propose to do to-day—and go to the celebration and carry my "hickory pole." God bless you.

July 6.—It has entered my mind to resume my letter to you, my son; and, that I may the better approach your understanding, I have not failed in the past day to read over many of your late letters to refresh my mind with your ideas therein contained. I am at present, and have been for half a century, a member of the Methodist Episcopal Church; and have, the while, tried, by God's assistance, to push forward the good work especially enjoined by His Son and blessed Saviour on all of His creatures here below. Of course I have fallen far short of my duty; at the same time I do not relish nor approve of your expressed views in regard to preachers and ministers of the Word. I do not fail to perceive that your mind inclines, but too strongly as I think, to draw invidious distinctions between religious sects, and to present more favourably the one than the other, and which, if you fail to take heed, may lead you into a distorted and biased line of thinking. It may be of acting also. You have divided all men into two classes, and it does appear to me that you have assigned all of Christianity to the one and none to the other, which is a task you nor any other human creature can do. You have not quite stated which class I may be placed in; and it is partly on this account I have thought it proper to inform you of the sect I belong to. Had the Church of England been extant in the wild and thinly-settled country it pleased God to introduce me in infancy, I have no doubt but that I should have attached myself to it instead of a reformed branch of it. At the same time I cannot consent to deny to other sects some good, mixed though it may be with evil. My advantages for historical reading have not been such as to enable me to form any definite ideas of "two classes" you dwell upon; and as I suppose you are indulging more of an abstract propensity, than treating of practical results, I will not discuss the subject of "classes," but leave you to follow the same as your mind listeth. I shall, the rather, notice the political results to flow from the classes you have made, and of which results you appear to have gloomy apprehensions.

I do not feel all of the apprehensions you seem to; yet I must confess I am not without serious misgivings in this matter. Complications in our Government appear to be increasing; wrangling and disputation are advancing apace, and seem to be leaving morality, wisdom, charity, and fraternity quite in the rear column as a kind of useless rear-guard. Instead of which these heavenly virtues should be in the front or leading column, and govern all our actions in public and private. Should this continue for a long time I fear the consequences for you and yours, though I should not be present to experience the same personally. I was born and raised in a slave State (Bottetourt, county Virginia), and yet I never owned any slaves; nor hath any of mine, so far as I know, ever owned any, unless a few have servants. I have not even employed any of the African race in any way. In fact, I have never felt the slightest inclination to give to the system, as practised of late, my approval. I do not say that I do not approve of servitude of the heathen races (whether African or any other) to a Chris-tian people; on the contrary, I do approve it—when done in the right way. Now, for that mode which is right, I go to the revealed Word of God, and there I find that it is absolutely commanded to go preach salvation to all heathens. Paraphrase it a little, and it may just as well read—" Go to, or bring to you, ye Christians, all the heathen of the world, and teach them the Word of God and the salvation of Christ." Now, I have tried to do what I well could to enlighten the heathen. I was almost the first white man to settle among the heathen Indians on the French Broad; and they used me roughly—had me prisoner—held councils over me, to put me to death, &c.

I failed not, and faltered not, in my firm convictions of my duty to teach and convert them to the ways of Life and of Light. But the system in operation among the Christians, of pushing the Indians back and away from the means of enlightenment and harmonising influences, rendered any efforts I might make futile to a great extent. Surely there is a dereliction in this matter on the part of all enlightened people in this country which must bring, at some period, a most fearful retribution. I feel this in my soul, and I tremble for the consequences. Not that I love the Indian, especially; but because I feel the end which God hath assigned him, and feel the conviction that I, and mine, are the appointed agents and stewards to lead him to that end. Have we done it? No; my son, we have not; nor any part thereof! Merciful God! Think of it! No part thereof, have we done! Now, precisely in this light stands the other class of heathens, the African negroes. No; I will not say in the same light. He stands in a far better condition, personally. Yet the aggregate motive of the Christians which places him so, I fear is of that sort which will fail of reward. I say, that I fear the motive which hath placed the heathen negro in a better condition than the Indian, while it does, and will continue to advance, in a measure, the purposes of God, to the Christianisation of the negro, will yet fail to secure to the owners the blessed rewards of our Heavenly Father. Now, it is not the ordeal of labour the negro is undergoing which ought to excite commiseration; it is not the restraints which his physical body is under that should call for relief; nor is it the corporal punishment which is uniformly inflicted which should be stayed. All opposition to these governing rules is misplaced philanthropy, and, when coming from well-informed men, savours of a hypocritical cant of the Scribes and Pharisees, and which hath another and a concealed motive. No; the heathen negro is just where he ought to be, so far as his daily labour is

concerned. The Indian were infinitely better off if he,
too, were in a like condition. Now I come to the practical abuse, and not the use of this system. The heathen
negro, as well as Indian, owes his time, and labour, and
efforts, and service to the Christian; and the former
is rendering it. But what does the Christian owe to the
heathen in return?—not dollars and cents. No. He owes
him, in due course of time, a Christian humanity. Is
that all, do you ask? Yes. And is that not enough.
Surely it is beyond price! because that is freedom indeed.
It is not only spiritual freedom, but physical freedom follows naturally. It requires no force, no interference, no
blood, no revolt; but it comes peacefully, gradually, and,
what is stranger than all, with magic acquiescence. Let
the Christian masters fully look this matter in the face,
and feel its truth and import, and they will tremble at
their awful responsibility, and speedily think less of dollars
and cents out of involuntary labour, and bestir themselves to a more rapid culture of the intellect, as well as
that of the physical. Without this culture the negro can
never be free. With this culture the Christian cannot be
induced to keep him in bondage. This may require
decades of time—even centuries. Let the northern anti-
slavery people think of this, and they will cease trying
to send weapons to inflame an ignorant heathen people
against Christians; which only tend to check enlightenment of mind, which has long ago been partially commenced, but which cannot be sufficiently advanced if this
recent interference goes on till the weapons of harm,
pushed through its channels, would work destruction.
Let the anti-slavery North people look over the wander-
ing tribes of Indian heathens, towards whom they have
woefully failed to do as God hath commanded; and if
they are right-minded they will tremble with visions of

a fearful retribution close at hand. Nay, they will say God speed you, brethren of the South, in your good work with the negro; but, I fear for the results. The North have sinned, and have almost entirely failed in this task. The South have sinned, and have not so failed in the results to be attained; but have turned the means and objects into a vile and damnable acquisition of worldly gain which hath most woefully retarded the end in view, while it almost divests them of the rewards due to good motives!

We are all bondsmen, some more than others, and we owe a debt of constant servitude to our God; and, while some of us are sufficiently enlightened to know by study and prayerful reflection what service is acceptable to Him, there are others, whose benighted condition extends even to bondage of a physical nature, and who must seek, little by little, the release from enthralment from intermediate sources and classes more advanced. I do not object to slavery; nor should any Christian man, North or South, object to the enlightenment in slavery or out of it; but I do object to many of the improper regulations governing it. These have a remedy in peace, but not in war! Those having it in charge are not doing their duty. It is a lease, or a trust, confided to us which must be performed, or the trust will prematurely expire, i. e., be forfeited; in the which both slavery and anti-slavery will be accounted as nought, but will both be engulfed in one sad ruin. May God help us to see things as they are. May God help us, and each and every soul, to cease these miserable sectarian animosities, and to cultivate faith and confidence in each other, and charity for each other, that we may, unitedly, set our hands to the work before us. There are those in the North who affect to see the sum of all infamy in a little speck of

bondage of a few poor miserable African heathens. Their
grounds for such are utterly false, ridiculous, and unworthy
of true Christians. I fear their motives are also false!
There are those in the South, holding these slaves only
for self-aggrandizement, and account such service of
eternal duration. The same beings! What folly. What
absurdity on both sides. Both are condemned of God!
Slavery of body and mind will exist as long as there is a
heathen on earth. It is God's own school for heathens;
and he who despises it, or he who perverts it to wrong
purposes, will receive like condemnation. I have not
time to read over what I have written. I have spoken
from the heart. My life is a long one; more than is
vouchsafed to many. As my duty is, so have I spoken
the truth as I do feel it.

God bless you,

GEORGE TURNLEY.

LETTER XVI.

Eagle Pass, Texas, June 30th, 1849.

YOURS of 30th ultimo has chased me from Austin to this
place. The object of my being here is, to locate a military
post at some suitable point on the Rio Grande—the new
boundary line between our nation and that of Mexico.
This spot we have selected as the one most favourable for
such purpose. I am therefore about two hundred and
seventy miles west of Austin, the capital of Texas, and
about fifty miles due west of the Nucus River, so much
referred to in Congress during the late war with Mexico.
You seem still to deprecate very much our increase of
territory, as furnishing grounds for serious apprehension
of future trouble. I do not think, however, that the mere

extension of limits can be considered cause for such, though it will certainly be made the means for developing the true cause, or motive, and which I have alluded to before. The line agreed upon between free and slave territory, at the admission of Missouri, and which pretended to be a compromise between the North and South factions, I see Mr. Douglass tried to extend from the Sabine (its western limit when agreed upon) to this river, the new western limit when Texas came into the Union; but he failed (see the proceedings in Congress relating to Texas admission). I wonder what will be the result now, since we have extended our limits entirely to the Pacific. The North faction opposed that compromise line in the first place, because they wanted more free territory, as they called it, and less slave territory. And I see that it is this same North faction who have opposed the extension of that line on through Texas. Of course, I presume they will continue to oppose its extension to the Pacific. Meantime, the South, I presume, will insist on it being extended. If this be so, we may expect another war of ideas, like that of 1821 and 1822. This is sure to follow any attempt to extend that line. Its formation, in the first place, was most unfortunate, and was a sacrifice of constitutional principle to expediency, which is always the seed that produces a heavy crop of troubles. But even Henry Clay was its author; and no doubt it was from good motives. He and many others saw then, and see yet, that Constitutions are flimsy, paper concerns; and, however much reverenced by some, are not, on that account, even known to or understood by others. It is evident, from present appearances, that the many questions of political differences in this country are going to be merged into some one of these differences, which may appear to be the most potent for attack and defence. To my mind this will be the

G

subject of free and of slave territory; and I must express
my belief that the South ought to be cautious not to insist
on any extension whatever, nor disturb the present status
of the line of slavery. I will give my reasons for this.
In the first place, its first establishment was wrong, and
did much to engender ill feeling; but the agitation of it
will only inflame that ill feeling. This would not be the
case, if both factions were really and truly contending for
a great principle; then there would be great moral honesty
and talent brought to its consideration on both sides.
But this is not the case. If the South contends for its
extension on purely constitutional grounds (and certainly
no man is so blind as not to see that the Constitution
does guarantee such, and in fact excludes the Congress
from the whole subject of making any such restrictions) then
they contend for a principle which is a mere abstraction.
On the other hand, the opposition to such, from the North,
contend for a practical result, namely, the limiting of
agricultural power and influence in the legislation of the
Government. This is a practical, tangible, and physical
element, to be seen, and felt, and handled; besides, it
has the whole North in its favour, which must override
the South in the end, on all these matters of political
expediency, or, if you please, of political economy. The
reason of this is twofold; first, the North is a " progressive
Democracy," and is, so to speak, a vast school of political
philosophers, or political economists. They reason from
false data, because all of their data are merely special
cases, cases applying only to their own community, and
hence are only true for a class or locality. What is good
for them is bad for others; what is best for them is worst
for others; what is their life is another's death. Yet the
North outnumber the South, two to one, and are daily
increasing, every new emigrant being one of this same

class of European-refugee "political philosophers," or "political economists," whom old nations seek to get rid of. I believe you claim to be something of a political economist, and hence will receive my strictures on that class of doctors with no very good grace; but, if you will agree with me in a definition of the term, I think you will be less sensitive on this point. I ask, therefore, what is political economy? It is not the science of government, surely, because the word, nor the field of its action, are yet three hundred years old, while civil government is thousands of years old. It cannot be the science which teaches men and nations fair dealing between each other, because it teaches opposite lines of action in different nations — even in different sections of the same nation (*vide* high tariffs taught in the North, *versus* low tariffs taught in the South). I go to the "political philosopher," again, for a definition, and after lopping off all verbiage, and flow of speech, I find that political economy "is the science which teaches one nation how to live on the labour of another;" teaches one community how to live on another community; teaches one man how to live on the labour of another man. Think of this a little, and you will certainly agree with me. Such, I say, is the definition and teaching of political economy now extant throughout the world; I don't say such ought to be its definition, or its teachings; on the contrary, political economy ought to be the science of fraternity. So ought religion to be the practice of Christianity, instead of, as it now is, the "school for hatred and infidelity." But, I am dealing with things as they are, not as they ought to be. Hence, political economy teaches the North how to live on the labour of the South, and teaches the South, in turn, how to live on the North, or at least how to avoid the burthen of supporting the North; that is, it teaches our antagonistic classes how to avoid each other's burthens, and how to inflict a burthen in return. It is the very science which first put on foot free competing labour, as the great boon, the acme of liberty, which I have heretofore said I conceive to be imaginary. Such, then, is philosophy, or political economy; yet this is the power which for three centuries has been striving to establish government on purely theoretical basis, regardless of God's laws, or the laws of Nature. Every word and line and precept of the political economist teaches man to compete with his fellow-man. It does not teach violence, bloodshed, and hatred. Yet it teaches the very mode of living and dealing which inevitably leads to blood and violence, places the goal to be attained to the strong or the cunning. It must, then, from pure consistency, acquiesce in the result, namely, that five out of six of the whole human family are the lawful victims, or slaves, of the remaining sixth. Our own country is too new, yet, for us to see much of the evil effects of this horrible doctrine, of which Thomas Jefferson was one of the advocates in the New World; but older countries, by their annual revolutions, by their pauper list, their almshouses, their numerous societies to relieve the growing wants of the five destitute, from the excessive accumulations of the sixth prosperous, demonstrate this result. God mysteriously (and wisely, we must suppose) so disposes the hearts of his creatures, that they naturally aggregate together, and counsel each other "how to relieve the wants of their fellows," although this want is, in fact, the bitter fruits of a warfare which political economists have put into action. We must accept this system of relief-societies as a means that God induces to correct or relieve evils which he hath permitted, not ordered or sanctioned.

But, to return to my subject—the twofold reason why

this territorial strife (should it come) will override the South. The one reason I have given—namely, because the North vastly outnumbers the South in votes, and is constantly increasing, and are all of that class antagonistic to Southern labour. I don't mean antagonistic to Southern slave-labour, because it is not true that political economists of the North can be opposed to slavery in the abstract; it is only in its temporary existence, because of its effects on Northern interests, mainly connected with Northern paupers, or the class corresponding to them in older countries. The North, *en masse*, are as hostile to the white labour in the South as they are to the black labour, just so far as that white labour is efficient. They oppose the black labour in loudest terms, only because black labour is the most potent. I wish not to be misunderstood on this point: I will, therefore, repeat what I desire to be clearly understood, which is this—the North people of the United States are not opposed to involuntary labour or service, in the abstract. I care not what they think they are, nor what they imagine their efforts tend to, or ought to tend to. In all this they may be as blind as possible, yet honestly so. But I mean to say that they cannot be, at bottom, opposed to involuntary service, according to certain fixed rules, for the reason that their whole efforts to relieve the wants of those who are in distress, by reason of free-competing labour, are directed (whether they know it or not) to the substitution of this involuntary service instead: hence, I say, I am quite sustained in asserting that the opposition of the North to the existence and extension of the exclusively African slavery of the South, measures the intensity of their underlying longing for involuntary service in the abstract, and in some shape for (the white as well as the black) man. Now, I am fully aware that the Northern philanthropist would feel shocked at this remark; but such is even the fact without his feeling conscious of it. He looks over the surface; and, urged on by the political economist from the old European nations (who has escaped to this country to inaugurate his revolution instead of in Europe), in this false idea of free-competing labour, thinks that relief to the five paupers I have mentioned, will come by the negro giving way to him; but this is false—relief will be only temporary,—but for a day. Just so soon as you fill up the State or city with three times the number required to do the labour, then comes the same competition, the same underbidding, to get the work. Needlewomen, who at first received fifty cents for making a shirt, because needlewomen were then scarce, get but ten cents a shirt when the supply is filled, and five over. But, say you, labourers will turn to various other vocations; so they will, but all vocations will soon be filled! Then what? Why, then begins want, hunger, crime, and poverty. Now, this does not result from the large number of people: it results from mean, selfish competition among them to out-reach, out-wit, and out-trade their neighbours, by which the earnings which would support all are concentrated into but few hands, which is taught and inculcated by those political economists of "free-labour-competition-schools." Then, you will ask me, what will you have? Will you have slavery every-where—as well white as black? My answer is, I don't know what slavery is; I don't know what you mean by the term "slavery;" and, one reason is, because I don't know what liberty is. I parted with what our country calls liberty when I entered the military service; I also parted with my power to pursue happiness in my own way—I yielded all, and am now, and have been for some time, the property of the President, who owns me, and orders and directs me, through his agents and his overseers, as he thinks best for the good of all. Yet, I don't call myself a slave; but I daily render involuntary service—service that I cannot escape from, because, if I do, some one else must take my place, which is the same thing. True, I am paid a certain price (not for my services, surely, because they are worth ten times what I get), but a price merely to feed and clothe me, in order that I may the better perform my duties for the President. You kept me in a similar state of involuntary service for twenty-one years, and paid me nothing but my feed and clothes. Now, I am not defending the word slavery, for I don't know what it means, in the great field of labour throughout the world; but I am defending the just and only practical relation of three-fourths of God's creatures to the other fourth, rendered reasonable, just, and humane by God's own laws of inferiority in size, mind, wit, moral capacity, &c.; and, on account of which, I denounce the war, and the strife, the wickedness, and misery of free-competing labour—*alias,* that the strong pluck the weak—should cease. I should prefer some other word than slavery. From my experience in a dependent service I should give it the name of "service of fraternity," or, "service of safety and comfort;" for such it is, and always will be, if the practical wants of mankind are consulted in enacting laws to govern the lord towards his vassals.

Encroachments of this kind, and based on this false idea of relief, will force the North over the South; unless the South take warning in time, and pursue the only practical method to avert it. She is not doing this now, and never has been. Her utter neglect of necessary duties to prevent this, forms the other reason why the North will succeed. The South is blindly contending for abstract principles, at a period and in a country where principles do not form the basis or motive for any action in Government legislation! The world hath its periods, since creation, as do the planets revolve. Practical applications of practical laws operate at one time; theorems *versus* practical rules operate at another. A confused, misapplication of philosophy, which is not, but is supposed to teach, utilitarianism, has full sway to-day in the United States. It is not to fortify negro slavery which the South should be employed at at this time. In another letter I will say what she ought to be at.

Affectionately yours,

PARMENAS.

LETTER XVII.

Sanantonia, Texas, December 30th, 1849.

I AM here on a brief trip for special purposes, and avail myself of the occasion to commit to paper my views on the duties of the Southern people and States, rendered doubly pressing by the grave aspect now presented in our Federal Congress of sectional enmity. I have thought over these relations seriously, and almost constantly; not in a spirit of prejudice, as you seem to think, but, if I know my own heart, my view of the whole is without bias or preference.

My last letter to you was dated June 30th, and from Eagle Pass (one hundred and ninety-five miles west of this). In closing that letter, I promised that in another one I would point out more definitely the course the Southern States should pursue. In the first place, let me briefly call to your mind the substance of my letters for the past two years. You will there find one leading idea insisted on: namely, that the whole world is divided into just two grand classes, which are antagonistic to each other—first in spiritual affairs, and secondly in all temporal affairs. Between these two classes there is, and ever has been, a conflict; sometimes of blood, and then merely of ideas. But ever and anon we find, clearly defined, two prevailing theories. I have also insisted on the fact that this antagonistic element is coeval with man's creation, and is spiritual in fact; so that all temporal disagreements are merely consequents, or means for the one or the other to attain the mastery. I have placed, as the most universal and constant of these means, or elements of temporal disagreements, the vocations of men; and I found that only two vocations existed on earth primarily; and that to one or the other of these two vocations belonged more or less intimately all sub-divisions, or branch pursuits. One of these vocations was that of husbandry, or agriculture in its broad and universal sense; comprising all creatures on earth, in whatever clime, who employ their time in cultivating the soil. The other class I call either mechanical, or that of the artizan; and in it I include all other people not included in the first. The first I have called those who create from the soil everything required for the subsistence of man and beast, and also everything out of which the artizan fabricates all of his products. Hence, for simplicity of treatment, we will say that the first class are exclusively employed in producing the raw material, while the second class are employed in transforming that material into the numerous useful shapes for variable and varying society, and in transporting the same wherever required.

Now, don't let your mind fix itself down on any speciality (as, for example, cotton, or tobacco, or hemp, or timber); I don't make any such limit, nor do I discover any such limit in the producer of raw material;

because the raw material of the ironfounder is as much
the product of the agriculturist as is hemp or cotton. So
also is the baling of cotton as much the work of the
artizan as is the spinning and the weaving it. Hence,
we will find at present in our time quite a mixture of the
two vocations—the same person doing a little of both
labours. But this is only an evidence of a very partial
blending of the two classes; not by any means an union of
them, nor a harmony of action between them. I have
also said that we have in the United States, more than in
any other country, these antagonistic classes, assorted out,
classified, and (so to speak) located in different latitudes.
There is, actually, no intermarriage or mingling of the
races. Each household has remained aloof from the
other in all domesticities, and, as a consequence of this,
the ruling elements of antagonism have been left free to
accumulate most intense power of opposition. Not only
this, but both classes have been drawing to itself only
those intense members of its own class: that is to say,
the North and the South people, diametrically different from
each other, in the first settlement on this continent, settled
apart from each other and pursued different vocations;
while each successive increase by emigration to either has
been from those extreme opposite classes from the Old
World. By this the South has received only that class of
its kind, and those of an extreme kind; while the North
has been the asylum only for the extreme elements of its
kind, which consists of the religionists, freethinkers, and
religious revolutionists of every nation in Europe. Thus
it is, then, that our nation, composed of the most diverse
elements on earth, are existing side by side, under a
paper bond, emblazoned on its pages, Fraternity! This
imaginary bond has so far proved peaceful; but there are
two other inscriptions now being written on that paper

by some of the extreme malcontents of France, Hungary, Poland, and England, and Germany, who have arrived in the North during the last half-century, which is to be the finality of Fraternity! and then, too, the finality of Union! These dreadful words, now being written, are " Liberty " and " Equality." Your paper bond will then be Fraternity, Liberty, and Equality! I have for years past, in all my letters, tried to prove my high appreciation of the first of these words—Fraternity. I love it. It is from Heaven, one of the essential attributes of him who shall make safe his calling and reach peace after this life. It is in the Scriptures called Charity; in temporal Government we call it Fraternity. But I cannot see how it can exist along with those other two words now being inscribed on its door-post! No, my dear father: I might as well order my tailor to make a "white-red-black coat," as to demand that Fraternity, Liberty, and Equality should live in the same household or in the same community, State, or nation. The God of Heaven hath decreed otherwise, in time and in eternity!

If Equality exists, it is the potent means—even the only means—whose sole mission is to destroy Fraternity; and it does it with amazing rapidity. If Liberty exists, which is utterly impossible,—yet, if the effort of man be to produce equal liberty, then is he at war with his fellow-man, with all creation, even with his Maker's works; for He hath made men and angels, and all creatures and things unequal, and, under classes and systems, subservient to each other, while all are subject unto Him. This effort to force an unnatural equality is the ammunition to carry on a war between antagonistic classes. It is covered, and cloaked, and concealed; it hath many stages to pass through, but its end and aim is Dominion! It will fail! But not without much effort, long suffering, and desolation. It is not new in the world; it is only new in our country. It hath always failed. So will it fail again; but not for some years, or decades yet to come. There is now a war between the North people and the South people of this nation; and composed of the antagonistic elements the same as exist in all nations, only they are more thoroughly asserted, and hence more intensified here than elsewhere. This war appears to be for this, for that, and yet for another object. But these are only apparent objects, not real. The motive is the same that hath led step by step from a war of ideas to a war of blood! So it will here in the end.

But this war may be deferred. It may be postponed or modified. The manner of doing this, in these United States, now rests solely with the Southern people. I say it rests solely with them, because nothing short of Divine interposition can produce any relief from it in the North. The North is hopelessly merged into a "religious demo-cracy," the elements of which are of the most extreme par-tizan advocates of an impracticable, visionary, leveling of dissimilar objects, and of blending antagonistic natures. Hence, nothing that human power or skill can do, will check or stay its course. But the South can modify, check, and restrain this current by timely action. This brings me to an unpleasant part of my subject, but a sub-ject which must needs be dissected. I have, in the course of previous letters, said much in commendation of Southern vocation or agriculture; and all I said I believe to be true. But you must not suppose that I have nothing to com-plain of. I have much; and it is to correct the evils of the same in the South that I now offer a few words of advice, which I hope you will not fail to scatter broadcast. The Southern people have been content to pursue the agricultural vocation to the exclusion of everything else.

This is wrong; and, unless it be speedily changed, will prove their ruin. Agriculture is the simplest of all vocations. It is the surest, yet slowest, to competency— slowest, because it has to enrich all others while it secures its own competency—the surest because it is peaceful and never fails. But its exclusive pursuit in the South has prevented the cultivation of any mechanical skill among the people necessary to render tenfold valuable her agricultural products. The wealth, therefore, which is in the raw material annually produced, is extracted in the Northern States or in Europe! and the man who produces that material out of Mother Earth only receives one dollar, where the North or Europe receives five dollars! Why is not your cotton made into thread and cloth where it is raised? Why is not your tobacco prepared in the States where it is produced? Why are not your ships and steamboats built along your sea-coast instead of the timber now there being sent a thousand miles North to be made into ships? Why is not your sugar refined where made, instead of in the North? Why not your hemp and flax made at once into rope, instead of paying freight on the crude and more bulky material? Why not manufacture the ten thousand articles of household comforts from the millions of acres of heavy timber now surrounding you, instead of sending to the North for all these? Why not open the unlimited fields of iron ore and coal beds, and make your iron ware, and all articles of the iron class at home, instead of procuring them in the North with high duties, and then pay freight on them for a thousand miles. As it is, a bale of cotton goes to Lowell at heavy cost of freight. It is there made into thread, then marked with cost, profits, tariffs, and then sent back to the very man who raised it to clothe his family! Just so with every other article I have men-

tioned. Can you conceive of greater folly or stupidity?
Still there is a deep, divine reason for this in first elements of nature; namely, the social, easy, live and let
live nature of the husbandman. And if all the world
were governed by like fraternal feelings, then even this
stupid course might not be the worst; but, as human
nature now stands, it is the height of all folly. But this
is not all the evil, nor the half of it; exclusive agriculture prevents education, because there is nothing in it to
exhibit the necessity for it, and necessity alone will produce results among men in temporal wants.

I have before intimated that the purest civilisation is
that of the Christian agriculturist. Now I come to say
that it is also the lowest civilisation. This you may think
contradictory, but it is not. The most highly educated is
also the most highly civilised. They may not be the purest
Christians, but their civilisation is always far above that
of the exclusive agriculturist. Hence, I ask why are not
the South filled with schools—free to all—without price
and without stint? No reason under the sun but that
the people confine themselves exclusively to the plough.
The consequence is the rich, and all who want education, go off to other countries to get it! and spend millions of money every four years elsewhere in sustaining
foreign Colleges which should have been spent near
at hand, where her whole population would receive the
benefit! Not only so, but this exclusive agriculture—
preventing the mechanical entirely—deprives a certain
class in all communities from embarking in that species ·
of labour they really prefer and have a taste for; and the
man who has surplus money to invest is forced to go
abroad to do it, instead of investing it at home in some
system of manufactories.

The result of all this folly is a constant drain on the

soil of the South to create five dollars worth of raw material, only one dollar of which stops with the producer, while four dollars lodge in a distant pocket! and the ploughman knows not education because he feels no need of it!

Now, that the South is in the condition I have pictured, is notoriously true. You all know it. The North knows it. The world knows it; and it is this condition, and the spirit and disposition of her people that sanctions its continuance, which constitutes her extreme weakness at this hour.

The Northern religious democracy say the South is in her present condition because of "Negro Slavery;" and a large portion of the North people, *plus* the same element of human nature in Europe, no doubt believe what they say; yet this don't make it true. I have shown that the North, and her similar natures elsewhere, are as false in theory as the South are in practice. The North say negro slavery is the cause of the South's present stand-still condition in schools and mechanics. If they could be induced to reason practically instead of falsely on this and other governmental points they would see the error of this. It would be more nearly correct to say that negro slavery in the South is the result of the spirit and genius of the Southern people. This is, in fact, true; and yet there is no earthly connection between negro slavery and want of schools, or want of mechanics. On the contrary, negro slavery really favours both schools and mechanics above all else. Because the heathen negro is fit only for the plough (at present, and for a century to come), and for the quiet domestic duties of the fireside; hence, this leaves all the whites free to attend schools, or to develop their higher genius in the mechanical shops. Is this not the plainest truth. Yes; but, says the North, negro slavery corrupts the whites, and degrades labour. This you know, and all men in the South know, to be a mere assertion without any truth. In fact, if it were true in the South to day, it must have been true in ancient periods, because slavery (not only of black but of all) was the rule, and freedom to the few was the exception. Yet we do not find that even white slaves made labour dishonourable, or white labourers degraded. Still less can African slavery have this effect.

Who were the mechanics and artizans of Rome and Athens? whom even inventive North and inventive Europe only partially imitate to-day! Down on such nonsense! That negro slavery degrades white labour in the South is as false as hell, and is known to be so by the shrewd partizan of the North who utters it. But it is not known to be false by nineteen out of twenty of his deluded, anxious, striving followers, whose morsel to eat, and that of his family, depends on his underbidding his neighbour in work of "free competition." So far from negro slavery in the South degrading white labour, the reverse is true, as millions of white men can testify who follow their ploughs daily. Your father never owned one, yet he followed his plough and defended negro slavery. You, his son, and seven other sons, who never owned a negro, have followed your ploughs in summer, and divided your time between the bar and the pulpit the rest of the year; yet you all bear testimony to the fact that negro slavery in the South does not degrade labour nor the whites, but elevates them. No! it is not negro slavery which degrades the whites of the South. In the first place, the whites in the South are not degraded; and he who utters it falsifies truth. It is a puritanical assertion for puritanical purposes. But the Southern white masses were thrown into a wide, extended country—a perfect wilderness, and with no means of communicating with each other, or with the more advanced portion of the world. They were, as a general thing, poor people, little else than a Christain faith to begin with, and they have failed to avail themselves of all the necessary means to make their labour as productive as their enemies and rivals have done. This has resulted, mainly, because they permitted the natural. effects of a purely agricultural life to lull them into an indifference to matters of education. Here is the root of the evil. Want of education degrades labour everywhere. Nothing else that I know of does degrade labour, except ignorance. I know of no conventionalities of a domestic kind in all my travels or reading or observation, which degrades labour, excepting it be ignorance; and I think it will be difficult for the partizan leader of the North, or any other country, to show, truthfully, that slavery is, or can be, the cause of a lack of schools. The want of schools in the South is traceable to other causes, perfectly independent of slavery, and causes which would have existed if no slavery had been there. The want of schools and colleges is a burning shame and a disgrace to the Southern people. I am prepared to defend the South in everything on earth that relates to principle, honour, integrity, and high moral Christianity; but in her gross dereliction to education I cannot defend her. I will denounce her statesmen, her judges, her divines, and her Governors without stint, and severely, for this great crime. The want of education of her masses of whites is dragging her down daily and annually, because it prevents her embarking more in manufactures. This lack of schools is attributed to wrong causes, namely, slavery—which, though a false cause, is yet one in which the great mass of destitute "free competing labourers" will lay hold of, as the drowning man does the straw, especially when urged so to do by the reckless partizan leader, and " religious enthusiast " full to overflowing of " Red Republican France " and " Infidel Germany."

Therefore it is, I say to the South—first, cease your effort, in and out of Congress, to defend negro slavery. It needs no defence; God will take care of that. Cease your effort to get slave territory; that will also come naturally. These are all false points of attack, and are threatened only as a means, not the end. Let the South go to work at once, as one man, in establishing schools and colleges, in building up her manufactories. Cease spending your money in the North, and in Europe; convert all your available ready money into machinery, and two or three entire crops of your farms into means of putting it into working order at home. Educate, and make mechanics and navigators of your whites, while your blacks follow the plough. Apposition (false as it is) to negro slavery will at once cease. This falsehood, that negro slavery retards your progress, has been drummed into your ears so long by designing men, that half of you have really got to believe it, whereas your difficulty is in something else. In all I say, I am not advocating especially negro slavery; certainly not that in its present shape. It has evils, but they can only be corrected by education of the whites. A certain amount of education among the negroes will make them far more valuable and happy than at present; but this cannot be done till the whites are far more advanced in education than they are. If the South will do this, then will they demonstrate the truth and efficacy of representative liberal Government. If they fail to do it, *then will the North destroy what you now have, in one rabid " religious Democracy."* Whatever may appear to be the side issues brought forward from time to time in this country, yet the great conflict to be waged henceforth is a conflict between enlightened, cautious representative Government, on the one side (South), against a leveling Democracy, or a religious Rationalism, on the other side (North), the primitive elements of which are antagonisms of nature, but the means for which are any and all expediencies which may be at hand, in each succeeding stage of its progress.

Affectionately yours,

PARMENAS.

LETTER XVIII.

Oak Grove, Tennessee, July 15, 1846.

I RECEIVED your letter of the 4th instant, and was glad to hear of your health and safe arrival. But I am not pleased at the views you express concerning our Government. Sometimes I fear you are too simple to be so far from home. Your Utopian notion of races, and the "antagonism of races," is an old falsehood which will never fail to have half-witted people to defend it. But I am grieved to think I have a son so short-sighted as to sympathise with such absurdities. Still more grieved to have one who can think so unworthily of his sires for having laboured in a long war to establish, and then in a second war, to perpetuate free Government. Time and experience, mixed with more study, will remove these clouds from your mind, and I shall have the pleasure of reading a recantation of all this from you at some future time. Meantime, see to it that you don't fail to perform your whole duties as an officer of that Government in which you appear to have little confidence of success. Although I wish some other than the military profession had claimed your attachment, still, like many other things,

H 2

the military is a necessary evil, and while I have no very high opinion of military men as a class, I hope they are more weak than wicked. I was in the War of 1812, and from good cause I formed the worst possible opinion of the head and heart of some who commanded over me, one of whom you now have in New Orleans (Gaines). I hope the fraternity has improved in the interim, and that long before your period for a final disruption of all our Government, we will have little or no use for your class of officers. As you say, your apprehensions of future troubles lie in the remote elements of men's natures, I hope in your dissertations you will not fail to go back far enough to "begin at the beginning," so that as I progress I will know that I have done with the subject.

Your grandfather is quite feeble—approaches his hundred years. He bids me say, that he fears your military studies have had the effect to warp your ideas of popular Government. In fact, this is one of the evils of a military institution. The military to be useful must be tyrannical, hence the anti-liberal notions engendered. You must resist this. Cherish the great virtue in Government of the popular voice, which is after all the only rule of Government, because it is the voice of those alone who are to be governed. Write me often, even though you persist in boring me with nonsense.

Affectionately,
J. C. Turnley.

LETTER XIX.

Oak Grove, May 20, 1847.

Yours of 15th ultimo from Vera Cruz came duly to hand, and gave me the first information of your sickness; but I am much gratified that it also contains the information that you were recovering. I hope, ere this reaches you, that you will be sufficiently well to visit New Orleans, and will thence consider it both a pleasure and a duty to extend your trip home. It is now nearly five years since we have seen you. Your grandfather is even more anxious to see you than the rest of us, if possible; while his great age scarce gives promise that he can count on living to see you at any very distant day, I do hope, therefore, that you will run up the river as far as Nashville, thence in stage to this place. From the sickness you have had, it is highly improper (if avoidable) for you to remain in that prostrating climate during a long hot summer. Thirty days up in this mountain air will do more to re-establish your health and strength then a whole summer in New Orleans.

I have received, and read with much interest, your several letters on the "political antagonism" existing in the United States, &c. Some of your views I agree with, but some others I think are very crude, and scarce containing anything warranting an application to our national affairs. The fact is, I am at a loss to understand whether you really entertain serious fears of difficulty, or whether you only want to vent your feelings of aversion to Democracy; if the latter, it will readily account for your laboured effort to abuse it; but if the former, then I scarce think your fears will ever be realized. I feel no little pride in having contributed, in the last War, to the aid of establishing the rights claimed under our present Constitution; so did all your uncles participate in the same, while your grandfather (now living, to read your letters) took an active part in the late and the first Revolution. It is needless, therefore, for me to say that none of us agree with you in your expressed views of imminent dangers in the future. It may be true that people of diverse characters and natures settled this country, and all participated in the formation of our present form of Government; yet, there cannot be any conflict of interest, still less of habits and manners, as I think which will warrant serious apprehensions for the future. Your great grandfather held much the same views you do, and even considered it his duty not to resist the laws and commands of the King and Parliament; but it was not because he failed to appreciate a just cause of complaint. It was because he had taken an oath, when leaving Liverpool for the New Country, that he "would never take up arms against the Sovereign," &c. Hence, as was natural, he endeavoured to excuse himself on the plea that all grievances could be more easily redressed in peace than in revolution. And in this he was certainly right. But, as you have rightly said, it was the design of the Colonies not to ask for a remedy under the old Government, but to establish a new Government, *de facto*. I think we improved vastly on the English Government. As a further proof of it, we have lived to see the English Government amazingly modified by the example we set them. Remove a few grievous errors still existing in that Government, and I could wish that ours possessed some of its more stable characteristics; still, I feel no doubt but that those who made ours can always preserve it. It was not formed in Revolution, as you and some others have intimated; it was fully organized and put in motion after the Revolution—in calmness, wisdom, and deliberation. It is not an absolute Government, but one of specific, well-defined, and divided powers. *The States are the units of the national Government,* and as such delegated certain powers (not uncertain nor indefinite powers, as you would imply). All uncertain or indefinite powers were, and are, lodged with the respective States.

These reserved powers are not the same either; but vary in extent and character, as do the several States vary in habits and manners, and can be exercised by the several States within their limits in a sovereign capacity, save and except only that such exercise must not run counter to the grants in the Federal Constitution, and the laws passed under it: hence, laws passed by the Federal Congress, regardless of that Constitution, *are void;* and, in order that all the States may have an uniform mode of ascertaining this fact, a supreme court is organised under that same Constitution, whose powers and functions are restricted also to the simple action of deciding the question when brought before them. They do not go round to hunt up questions—they merely act when the question is carried to them: hence, when that Constitution is so express in its own powers and limitations, and a special court has been created for no other purpose than to explain it, surely I fail to see the point of " antagonism " in our political organisation, whatever may be in your " classes of mankind." " Government," in the true sense of the term, on this Continent was commenced, and has been carried on, always, *in States*—not as a national one. The practical and theoretical workings of all civil Government in this country, I repeat, is a purely State affair. The national feature is an after agreement, and for a specific purpose only, and, I will add, a very limited purpose, and which is too well defined for any State, or number of States, to attempt to overstep the limit.

However, when you arrive here, we will talk over these matters more fully. Until then, at least, we are all safe.

Affectionately,

J. C. TURNLEY.

LETTER XX.

Washington, November 30th, 1852.

SIR,

Yours of October 30th ult. has been read, and I
avail myself of the first leisure moment to reply. I feel,
as you do, full of apprehension concerning our political
relations ; and I know that my heart inclines to do all I
can to avert the evils threatened. But what can be done?
This is the question. If we had only to meet ordinary
difficulties it were easy; but we have to meet extraordinary ones. If we only had to provide for our
political necessities, with all hearts disposed to acquiesce
in "well enough," then could we readily see our way
clear; but, as it is, a large portion have their hearts
turned to revolution, no matter what may be the patriot's
action. I have already tried my utmost to have the old
compromise line of 1820 extended, first to the Rio
Grande, then to the Pacific; but it was voted down by
the very party who opposed strongest its first adoption in
1821 ! This, you will say, is extraordinary. I say so,
too; but it is true, and only proves how perverse, how
wicked the hearts of some among us are ! My plan now
is to bring forward a Bill to repeal altogether that compromise. This is what you suggest. I have tried the
extension of it, and have failed. I am now for its repeal.
It was a compromise of principle in the Constitution in
the first place, which was wrong; yet it was acquiesced in,
and for that reason I was willing to continue it. But I
am met in my efforts by the most violent opposition from
Northern fanatics ; so I will try to remove altogether the
question, and we will thus very soon be able to give form
and character to the extensive domain you refer to. It

is large enough for three or four territories, and we will certainly make two, or perhaps three, out of it in the first place.

I received your previous letter on the subject of Commercial Power *versus* Agricultural Extension, and I am quite of your opinion. I do not believe that those people who are so loud in their opposition to slavery are honest. I do not believe that they really dislike slavery *per se*. On the contrary, I am frank to confess that they appear to me more and more every day as the covert, sly enemies to white men's liberties, far more than they are friends to negro's freedom. The misfortune is, too few among us thus closely watch their designs; and the danger is, they will get power, under false pretences, when it will be too late to prevent the ruin they have fully meditated on the country. I do not find all of these elements of destruction from the North! I find some of the most cunning, subtle, and treacherous of them to be from the so-called Slave States originally. These men are more to be watched than all others, because they are false as hell, and have their hands ready to receive their price! Illinois has several of this class; so has Missouri, and Kentucky.

My efforts have always been, and will continue to be, for the best. I have no guide but my heart and my judgment. I had rather be the means of averting the dreadful calamities we both see and dread, than to hold all the offices under Government. Any honest man can perform the duties of office; but it takes also sagacity, effort, courage, and faith, to meet the enemies of popular Government. By this I mean the enemies to our plain Constitutional Government. You justly remark that we have no Government outside of the Constitution; and if that durst be violated with impunity, and persisted in, then are all parties who come together under it absolved from further adherence to the Government. As to how far such violations should be borne before a withdrawal by States, I cannot say. This will of necessity depend on the feelings of those who suffer by the breach of faith. I could hope, however, (and I feel sure such will be the action), that a call for a general Convention of all the States will precede any hasty action by separate States. This would rouse the latent patriotism in the North to strangle at once the enemies to Constitutional Government, who have been permitted to grow and increase unmolested the last half-century.

The South is certainly becoming very weary of abolition flings at their States and their domestic relations. Still, I have confidence in their patriotism to suffer it still longer; for I do believe the Southern people, rich and poor, are the most devoted people to Constitutional Government on earth.

*   *   *   *   *

Very truly yours,

S. A. DOUGLASS.

LETTER XXI.

New York, September 1st, 1852.

MY DEAR FATHER,—

My last letter (dated on the extreme frontiers of Texas the past summer) scarcely intimated that I would so soon be addressing you from this metropolis. However, thus uncertain are all our goings and comings. I have availed myself of the opportunity to revisit the national school at West Point, and as I wrote you from

New Orleans to try and meet me here, I was in hopes you could have done so; because I was exceedingly anxious that you might visit also that valuable military school. West Point has its enemies as well as its friends; and what is strange, its bitterest enemies are those living in the old Eastern states, whose young men have received the greatest advantages from that school ! This is truly a strange feature, and is difficult to explain. You, at one time, felt some little enmity to that institution, but finally yielded to Jackson's reasons for its support, and I believe you have ever since been found defending it. Some oppose that institution on one ground, some on another; but the most usual grounds of objection put forward are that it is expensive, aristocratic in its tendencies, and fosters an established military system not friendly to the national militia. Will you excuse me, now, if I express the conviction in my mind that this dislike to the national school springs from the spirit of " progressive Democracy" now so rapidly overrunning the whole Northern and Northeastern States, and which is the poison destined to ruin this country. Whatever the retired citizens of these United States may think on the subject, I know I can speak for the thousands who have received diplomas from it when I assert that it is pre-eminently a national and nationalising institution. Without it there would certainly be much room to fear the effects of separate State military schools in the future; but with its nationalising influences spread broad cast over the whole country by its constantly receiving graduates representing every State in the Union, all fears of State schools are at once banished. West Point demonstrates most effectually its national character in the unmistakable effect on the minds of all young men who receive there their education. Not only so, but that school also gives the most wonderful proof

of the sad, sad character of most of the systems of education now extant throughout the country. The Northern
States stand to-day pre-eminent, in public estimation, for
their wide-spread system of mental education; yet it has
most glaring defects when brought to the test of West
Point proficiency; and while it thus exposes a great
defect in the education of the intellect, it shows a still
greater defect in the education of the heart in the present
schools of the North. On the other hand, as tested by
West Point, the South is tenfold more deficient in her
education of the intellect, yet more efficient in that of the
heart. One-half of all the Southern and South-western
young men fail at West Point because of a deficiency in
early education; this deficiency being the direct result of
no system of home schools. On the other hand, those
from the North are over-crammed with a purely mental
culture, by rote, by the book, and by rule. These ruinous
defects only become apparent to the close observer when
all sides are brought together at this national school.
The nation will receive a great wound the day partizan
leaders succeed in abolishing West Point; not only in a
political sense, but in a moral and genuine scholastic
system of education. If the North would dispense with
one-half of the present hot-bed, forced culture of the
mind or intellect, and give more attention to the moral
and to the cultivation of the hearts of youths, and the
South would quadruple the efficiency of her home schools,
the country would be in safer hands ere long.

While on this subject (of education), I will recall to
your mind what I said in previous letter last year touching the matter of education in the South. I there stated
that the great lack of education in nearly all of the South
was a burning shame; that every white child ought to be
not only supplied with a complete education free, but

each and every one ought to be compelled by statute to receive the same.

But, it is proper for me to say that I do not recommend the system of mental culture in the South, which obtains now in the North; on the contrary, very much of that extant in the North should be avoided. The North directs too much to specialities—too much to special vocations, with a view to a specific profession, or trade. This may do very well for any one trade, but, by excluding so much else, it becomes very injurious to the body politic. Besides, from the greater opportunities which the whites in the South have for going to school, they ought, as a mass, to become more thoroughly educated. With all the boasted perfection of the system for education in the North, I think I see something very wrong. It is not unusual to find young men in the North who have been going to school from five years old to eighteen or twenty; yet they are scarcely equal in education to our greatest men, who could only attend school three months in the year for five years. It appears to me evident that respite from books, by other labour, is very necessary; but this is difficult in the North, where there is nothing for such class to do. Not so in the South. Agriculture is universal, and actually supplies, at one's home, all the advantages of manual-labour-schools, where boys can pursue their farming in summer, and their books (in free schools) in autumn and winter. The North violates her progressive Democracy theory, in this matter of education, by removing it from "do as you please"—*vox populi* doctrine— and making it a matter of State law and authority. The South violates her law and order theory, by leaving education "to whom can," and "do as you please." The South must change this to a matter of State requirement. We live in the world for nothing, if we go out as ignorant as we came in. The purely agriculturist will do this, unless he be forced to education in the first place : once thoroughly started, however, it will thrive on its own productions. Education will at once beget a spirit of mechanical inquiry, which will be the very field to absorb the surplus white talent in the manufacturing shops, iron founderies, and sea-going labour. The South has always left this to chance : if she continues to do so much longer she is gone. I alluded to this in my letter on manufactories in the South, and need not here repeat it. Further, then, to say that the Southern people will be poor until they cease sending away the raw material of their farms, to be made up in distant States or nations. I know your panacea for all this is free trade : I am also for free trade, but for this purpose. I am not for free trade as a remedy for the poverty of a purely agricultural people : it will never bring any relief. The relief it brings is only temporary, and that to the few cunning ones, who can take advantage of it.

It matters not to what nation you pay duties, if you continue to pay. High tariffs, in our country, favours home manufacturers, by enabling Eastern mills to work up the raw material. Cut off this tariff, and the only difference is, the raw material would not go East, but would go direct to Europe. True, you would, for a time only, receive a little more of made articles for your raw material. You might get a little more railroad-iron for a bale of cotton, or a few more bolts of prints for a hogshead of tobacco. But even this would soon be taken advantage of by that more distant manufacturing community you dealt with. No; the only remedy—the only safety of a purely agricultural community, is in making up her raw material closer at home, " where the soil which produced it will receive back the 'dung' requisite to reproduce the same article." You then get your five dollars among the home people, instead of one. Your bedsteads, wash-stands, ploughs, wagons, carriages, coaches, are made from the timber round you, and by your own surplus white mechanical skill; while your cotton which was picked yesterday, is put into thread or cloth without even baling! Your railroad-iron is being made almost along the very route where it is to be laid, and not brought from Pennsylvania nor yet from Liverpool. All this would follow speedily were a moderate number of the wealthy men in the South to start up their own manufactories. Do you tell me that means are wanting? Then, I ask, where is your annual exports of two hundred millions of dollars? How many men are there in each State worth half a million of dollars, one half of which, at least, could— without even temporary detriment to his business—be at once invested in manufacturing? But the will is wanting! That is all. The day will come when the people of the South will see, either their folly in neglecting this, or else the necessity of going at it.

But I have wandered quite off from the subject I began to write about. To return to that, I will make one more remark, which is—that the fictitious, poisonous, and false education of the intellect in the North, and the utter want of education in the South, is fast ruining this nation ; because it is placing the political existence of the nation in the hands of the destructive revolutionists of all Euro-pean nations—who come here because they can't practise their destruction at home!

Affectionately,

PARMENAS.

LETTER XXII.

Salt Lake City, Utah, May 30th, 1860.
DEAR FATHER,

I am very thankful for your kind offer, in applying to Mr. Floyd for a leave for me, useless as such application is at the present time, and especially for me; Floyd evidently identifies me with the "chief" in this territory, and hence considers me his special enemy; and, however false this supposition, still, it will have the same effect; I have forwarded my resignation, and 'shall wait till my successor arrives, and relieves me of all property and money. I will then quit a service which has about ceased to be honourable. I hope that Mr. Floyd will at least order all my accounts to be closed, and accept my resignation. The political clouds on the horizon suggests to every military man the propriety of freeing himself, without delay, from all cumbersome surroundings, so as to be free to choose such course of action as events may require. I am sorry that the people in Tennessee are so stupid, luke-warm, or indifferent; they seem to neither care nor think of those difficulties in the future, which I have so often alluded to in my letters for the past ten years.

By the way, have you read the recent speech of that man, Mr. H. Seward, of New York? If not, you should read it at once, and let every man read it who has a speck of common honesty. No honest mind can read it without seeing the cunning, and dark and damnable scheme at the bottom, and in fact, a full, complete, and perfect programme for the destruction of the American Government, such as I wrote you about from Nebraska in 1856 and 1857.

It will be refreshing for you people in Tennessee, who follow your ploughs, and all other daily labour, to hear

Mr. Seward call you Capital States, and in the next breath call the New England States Labour States. I think this is certainly the most transparent libel on truth that a shrewd man has ever been foolish enough to utter. Still, Seward has the Puritans with him; and, because of Puritan capital holding the meat and bread of millions in the North in their own coffers, these millions have no other alternative but to fall in with Seward's false theory, and train in his company.

When one looks over the South, and seeks in vain to find any capital whatever, but meeting nothing, save labour at every turn, every hearthstone and cottage, truly may we wonder that the very opposite should be asserted of that poor country. Still more strange is it, that, with nothing but capital in the Puritan States (including a large part of New York and Pennsylvania), the same man should assert that those States are "Labour States." God save the ignorant, I say, in these "last days" (as Brigham Young says)!

Mr. Seward and Co. mean to destroy the Government of the United States, for he has said so, in social conversation, a score of times, and he will effect it ultimately. The very blanket with which he covers his work is this profession of love for it.

I had prepared a condensed description of the Mormons and Utah, which I designed for your information; but press of business has prevented me from finishing it entirely; besides, there is at present (or has been) so much morbid curiosity, mixed with so much ill feeling, throughout the country, in regard to Mormonism, in Utah, that I thought I would let the manuscript lay over till the public mind became more calm. I shall, however, try to finish it up, and let you have it. I don't suppose that one in a thousand in Tennessee ever heard of a Mormon, or

I

has the most distant idea of what the fraternity consists of. All this you and they (as many as care to read it) will learn from my few pages on the subject, which shall be forthcoming in a few weeks more. It is short, and to the point; avoids personal opinions, excepting as to a few points; gives the character of that "class" which compose the "Mormons." This must needs bring into it "religious classes," which (in the United States) compels one to class them in a political light. You will, no doubt, take issue with me, in some of this classification, but you have done this so often, that I have become quite used to it.

Affectionately yours,

PARMENAS.

LETTER XXIII.

Omoho City, Nebraska, August 25, 1855.

*   *   *   *   *   *

I WROTE last month of the organisation in the Eastern States for the purpose of driving all Southern agriculturists out of this and Kansas territories. This organisation is being rapidly perfected, and is on a most extensive scale. I have met several of the leaders of this party and they are being rapidly and amply supplied with all the means—both in money and arms! An old scoundrel, by name of Brown, with several sons or nephews, from some interior county of New York, heads the crowd; and a large number of Puritan Congressmen, and half a-dozen Senators, and a dozen preachers are the local resident agents in the Eastern States to collect contributions of money, arms, &c., and forward the same to this frontier! Take it altogether it is the most serious and extensive revolutionary organisation I have yet known of.

Its object purports to be on behalf of the negro, but I have learnt enough about it to know that it is really for plunder and robbery on the frontiers of Missouri and Arkansas, and to extend to Texas. It is a kind of a John Murrel* organisation on a large scale, with Eastern Senators and preachers to back it up. Some person or persons in East Tennessee, near to you, are also members of this infernal band. I can't learn who he is, but he is a methodist preacher, or exhorter, and lives in or near Knoxville; from all I learn, however, I think he is not a native of that State, but comes from some New England State; I wish I could learn who he is.† Holding out to the unsuspecting the idea of philanthropy, while, in fact, it is to steal and rob, and ultimately to revolutionise the Government. My advice to all Southern people, whether negro owners or not, would be not to emigrate to Nebraska nor Kansas. In the first place, not one-half of them will like the country; and, in the next place, it will not be a quiet and agreeable region to live in for many years to come.

I will here repeat what I have said for ten years, namely: the Southern people are fooling themselves in contending for constitutional rights in their negroes, because their opponents and enemies in the North know just as well as do the South all about these constitutional rights. But they don't care a farthing for such rights, nor for the Constitution either. Neither do they care, really, to free negroes. What they want to do is to revolutionise the American Government so as to strike a blow at Southern agriculturists, and get more control of Northern labourers and artificers, no matter whether they be negro-owners or the followers of their own ploughs. I know

* John Murrell is known, in Mississippi history, as the Great Land Pirate. He died in the States prison in Nashville, Tennessee.

† Perhaps Horace Maynard.

you have different views; but I know better than you do, because I have been sixteen years among the Northern Puritans and the emigrants from foreign countries, all of whom are of the radical revolutionary kind, and I have made it my business to learn quietly all about them. This old man Brown and his clan, consisting of his sons, and a fellow named Stevens or Stevenson, another named Cook, and Thompson, besides half-a-dozen more, have a secret rendezvous in Iowa, some fifty miles below here, and they are already doing much mischief. Brown has a regular correspondence with wealthy men in the East. Old Gerrit Smith, of New York, is really his agent. I am on very good terms (on the sly) with some of these infernal scoundrels, and therefore learn a great deal about their affairs and designs, which I would not get if they for a moment suspected my true sentiments.

I communicate this to you to be used for the benefit of innocent emigrants to Kansas from your section of Tennessee, and, also, for the true interest of the Government. However, you think that I am a sensationist, and therefore you must wait the advent of things before you can credit my views. This you will see before long. In the meantime, I wish to God the Southern people would cease to even mention the word negro, and would at once go to work to prepare themselves—in every State—to defend and protect, not negro slavery alone, but their homes and firesides! The time will come when the Christian people of the South will be most glad to be able to do that—and let the African go to destruction if needs be.

Affectionately yours,

PARMENAS.

LETTER XXIV.

March 14th, 1854.

*   *   *   *   *

POLITICALLY, the country (as you must see) is in no very promising condition. You will have seen by proceedings in Congress, that Mr. Douglass, in January last, as Chairman of Committee on Territories, reported a Bill for the organisation of the Territories of Nebraska. On the 23rd of same he offered another, making two territories—one called " Nebraska," the other to be called " Kansas." The latter, Kansas, is west of the Missouri River, east of Arkansas, and runs out nearly to the Platt River, but terminates at the junction of the Platt River with the Missouri River. Nebraska begins at the mouth of the Platt River, and extends up, on the west side of the Missouri River, indefinitely. Kansas is a fertile region of country, and a good climate ; Nebraska is good soil (on the Missouri River, and other smaller streams), a most healthy, but is a cold climate. Few, if any, from the South will care to emigrate there; but they will, no doubt, like that of Kansas. I have been all over both regions of country, and am perfectly familiar with the character of water, soil, timber, grass, &c., and will gladly give to those desiring it, all requisite information.

Much difficulty awaits the country in the future as to negro serfage and freedom in these territories. Mr. Douglass has tried to avoid this for ten years : first he tried to extend that old Missouri compromise line of 1821 to the Rio Grande, when we acquired Texas ; but the Northern Puritans prevented it. Douglass then tried to extend the same to the Pacific, at the time we acquired California by treaty with Mexico, some time in 1848 or 1849. The same Puritan element prevented it. Finally, as California, New Mexico, and Utah, had to be organised in some way or shape, Douglass assented to some legislation in 1850 and 1852 (for New Mexico and Utah), which really abrogates the old Missouri compromise! This was not discovered by the Puritans till very recently; and Douglass, in his late Bill, in order to set everything like a misunderstanding out of the question, expressly annuls that old Act, and thus leaves the people of these new territories to decide the matter of negro serfage or no serfage, as they think fit. This, of course, is opposed by all the Puritans on, so-called, holy grounds; while, also, some Southern Churchmen oppose it because of fear that it may produce trouble. The Puritans here denounce Douglass in the most bitter terms; have burned him in effigy; posted dirty handbills in the streets; call his two children negro babies —you will recollect his wife, now dead, was a North Carolinian.

You have no idea of the venom and intense hatred of a Puritan. I will not attempt to describe it. If you have failed to see any of it in my previous letters these ten years, it were idle for me now to attempt to describe it. Suffice it to say, that the Southern people will know it by experience before another decade is past !

But I am sorry to see Southern Christians thrown off their guard so far as to be defending their rights to take negro serfs into territories. By this they are burning daylight, and only strengthening the Puritans. Besides nearly all the German revolutionists are now falling into the Puritan ranks. The Southern Churchmen were blind, very blind, when they came to the rescue of foreigners, and opposed the secret order of " Know Nothings" or native Americanism, in the North. A Mr. Seward, of New York (a senator, too, and who has made a long speech against the Douglass Bill, is really the originator of that order; and he is the most subtle, refined, political hypocrite I ever knew. The Southern statesmen, I think, fail to see the feints and false manœuvring which is being carried out against agricultural interests and extension. Not less deceived are the poor labourers of the North. The moneyed lords of the North, who are now prating for the negro, don't care a cent for him, really; but they must have more control over the poor artificer in their factories. The only way to get this is to cripple agriculture, or, which is the same thing, get the negro freed from labour, and on an equality with the poor white; then they will control both. I would like, above all things, to see half a million negroes sent into the Puritan States, and even into the North-western States; because, as self-interest governs all, I think these German infidels would soon find that Cuffey, freed, will soon reduce their wages.

At present, you can't hire a white man to plough here for less than one to two dollars per diem. This is owing to the fact that new land is all ready and labourers are few. It would certainly be good for the owners of negroes to get ten dollars per month, and have them fed and clothed, which would not exceed half a dollar a-day, all told. However, this we cannot see. The present plan must go on. The Puritans are now engaged in poisoning the minds of the "imported sovereigns," who glory in the name of "Democracy;" and, when all is ready, the now unsuspecting South will find out what a Puritan's love consists in. You read in the Northern papers that the Puritans hate slave-owners only. This is another smart trick to take in the non-slave owners of the South! But the Puritan's love, or respect for even a non-slave-owner

of the South is about one-tenth that of Judas Iscariot for
his Saviour.   The Puritans will love anything—the Devil
himself—provided it " pays," either in ready cash or political power.   They will hate anything—even Christ—if he
stands in their way of ready cash or of political power.
They will receive either of these articles in payment,
because they always have an eye to converting them into
long bonds.

But I will close by requesting you to read the debates
on the Bill.   Above all, read Wade and Chase, of Ohio;
Sumner, of Massachusetts; and, lastly, that arch-hypo-
crite, Seward.   I know him well.   Read his sophistry!

Yours truly,

Parmenas.

LETTER XXV.

Upper Missouri River, Nebraska Ty.,
August 20th, 1856.

Dear Father,

Your long letter of inquiry reached me some two
hundred miles from here on the head waters of the Big
Sioux River, and I have not had time to answer it till now.
I am just off a long trip, and will start in a day or two
still on another to establish a post somewhere below here
on this (Missouri) river.   I presume it will be at or near
the mouth of the River " L'eau qui Cour," or better known
by old folks as the " Neabrara."   I will write you more
about this when I get there.   Meantime, to your questions : you ask me who J. C. Fremont is.   It would
scarce be polite for me to enter into any extended bio-
graphy of him, as I never made his personal acquaintance;

but, as he married old Bullion's second daughter, you ought to take some interest in him, as you were one of those worshippers of Benton for so many years. Hence, you must not think me personal if I fail to tell you all I know and have heard about Mr. Fremont.

J. C. Fremont came into the United States' Army as a Lieutenant of Engineers about 1838. He is, I believe, from South Carolina : was a poor boy, and received much aid (as I learn) from the Catholic sisters in his early education. He received at a later date, from or through Mr. J. R. Poinsett's aid, a position in the navy; thence into the army. He continued a Lieutenant of Engineers; and while such "stole away" old "Bullion's" daughter. which made the old man and woman very angry. Like most parents under similar circumstances, however, they got over their anger, and set about doing all they could for the young Lieutenant and his wife. Hence followed Fremont's "gasy" trips over the plains, and the Rocky Mountains; his explorations, surveys, routes, &c., &c.; all of which were concocted by old Benton for Fremont's special benefit, and also to satisfy Benton's long desire to know more of our North-western regions. Hence it was that "My Son-in-Law" was well fitted out (having such a good parent at Court). He took draughtsmen, geologists, botanist, naturalists, and a thousand other *et ceteras*, regardless of expense. The result of all his travels has been presented to the world by a munificent "Uncle Sam," which (if you have nothing else to do) you might, perhaps, read a few pages of; but I think you will get quite all needful information in half-a-dozen of my letters while passing over the same country. Finally, in 1845, when it was "54-40 or fight," and Congress passed a law raising a regiment of rifles, J. C. F.'s "friend at Court" procured him the commission of Lieutenant Colonel of that regiment (Fremont being at the time out on, or near, the line on which it was intended this regiment should be posted). Thus it was he made a leap from a Lieutenant to a Colonel; but the Mexican war prevented the sending out of that regiment, hence Fremont remained out there on duty with other troops; got into trouble by claiming to command over his superiors; got put in arrest, was exceedingly insubordinate, finally was even mutinous, and so that General Kearny had to put him in close confinement. He was brought to Washington in arrest, and there tried before a Court and dismissed the service; but Mr. Polk saw fit to remit the sentence, and ordered him to duty; whereupon he resigned, and became, as did the whole Benton family, the inveterate enemies of the whole United States' Army. Finally, through the ramifications of the dark-lantern organisations now extant in the Northern United States. He was put up as candidate for President, where you now find him.

I don't suppose you have asked me so particularly about him because you entertain any idea of voting for him. Still, he is about as worthy as the usual run of partizan leaders now preying upon and devouring the vitals of the United States North. Fremont is "nobody-in-general," and "especially nothing," when you come to statesmen. For that reason I think he may get a pretty large vote in the Puritan States, because he is "always available" for "proper considerations." As to his parentage I know nothing; but I have heard it said that it is a wise child who knows its father. This I have heard from officers of the army—not that I know anything of him myself, and I certainly care very little.

Now, having answered your questions, permit me to express the hope that what I have said will not be made the subject of public political gossip for electioneering, or any other purposes; because, in the first place, such things do much harm, and no good, and is the very sin of the North Puritan States at this time; and I should rather not be the medium of following their example in this low, vulgar system of telling all you have heard.

Affectionately yours,

PARMENAS.

LETTER XXVI.

Chicago, Illinois, October 30, 1852.

S. A. Douglass, Washington.

DEAR SIR,

*   *   *   *   *   *

The country south-west of the Missouri River, which must very soon call for some kind of organised Government, lies above, that is, north of the old compromise line of 1820, and is evidently included in the compromise of 1850, which latter appears to do away with that of 1820, in case of admission of Missouri. Cannot that line be agreed upon still as the compromise line, and to be extended on to the Rio Grande, or to the Pacific? It will prevent a vast deal of future trouble in the legislation of our country. Utah has slaves in it, by compromise of 1850, merely by the will of her people; so ought other territories to be allowed to decide this. I have been for several years in the region of country I refer to—from north-east corner of Chiuahua to Yellow Stone. Government must be very soon organised in nearly all parts of it; and, knowing as I do, that the real aim of abolitionism is not to free negroes, but to curtail agricultural territory; and that the pro-slavery idea is not extension of slavery, but extension of agricultural territory, I hope both parties will agree, either to let the compromise of 1850 extend over this new country, or else let all (including Utah and New Mexico) fall back on that of 1820, and let the same be continued, as that of common agreement. Should this not be the case, I fear that extreme partisan spirit and action will be the result.

If this kind of spirit gets up just now, it will ruin the Government. We really have no Government—we have only a kind of "common-consent free territory," bound by good faith and a feeling of justice. Break this sentiment, and our Government ceases to be a unity at once; while party hatred will still try to inflict all the punishment possible, and a bloody war must be the result. Now, any hostility, no matter how little, must be the end of this Government.

I am going back to Council Bluffs, and hope to learn that this "idea" in territory, covered up, as it is, by the "word" (not the fact) of "slavery," is abandoned. I feel sure you will do all in your power to quell this sectional spirit. If it be not settled one way or another very soon, then is the end of our experimental Government already visible.

Nearly all of the territory adjoining Arkansas is agricultural, up as far as the mouth of the Sioux River, in Minnesota. Of course it becomes a rather cold region after you get above the Platt River; still it is a good soil and prairie, with timber on the Missouri River, and other smaller water courses.

Should fanaticism and wickedness refuse to apply the law of 1850, refuse to extend the old line of 1820, then why not repeal it altogether? It must either be acquiesced in, and thus extended, or it must be repealed: the former is good in practice, the latter good in principle:

hence, I think either, if agreed to, will suffice—at least, for a time; but, with the present damnable spirit of Radicalism, I don't look for peace very long.

Very truly yours,
P. T. T.

LETTER XXVII.

Oak Grove, Sept. 30th, 1848.

I RECEIVED yours from the city of Mexico, giving me the general news of peace, and something of the terms of the same, which, as I feared, includes that of a large addition to our already extensive domain. I have aided all I could the carrying on of the late war to a satisfactory close, but not for conquest. I suppose the acquisition of territory, in the treaty, may not be called conquest, because it is merely an indemnity for our great expenditure in prosecuting the war; still, I fear the result of this will be fruitful in trouble. I have read your several letters, lastly, one to your grandfather. You say so little about your views concerning our Constitutional Government, that I don't know whether you know anything about it or not. Sometimes I fear you are utterly ignorant that we have any Constitution at all. I am surely at liberty to think so, because you deal so much in abstract theories and antagonism of races, and on this antagonism you base the failure, or at least disruption of our Government, not even saying a word about the written character of the same; in fact, I begin to fear that your seven years' sojourn in the North has done you serious injury, and that you have imbibed the bad, to the exclusion of all the good. In the first place, then, we have not got a Government which exists by chance, nor yet terminable at the pleasure of a

" mob," (which you please to call " Democratic masses," I
thank you for the epithet, as I choose to be, in the true
sense, a Democrat; but I will say, that I have yet to discover that it possesses any of the mob spirit about me).
Our Government, then, is one of specific, legal statute, so
to speak, and if everybody don't understand it, it is because
they don't read it and study it. The contribution of the
several States to a Federal fund (called the Constitution)
was specific, and made the Federal Government all it was,
and all it is, and all it can ever become. It matters not
whether such be good, bad, or indifferent; it matters not
whether this Federal machine suits the North, South, the
East, or West; it is just what it is, and is nothing more, and
nothing less. The Federal Government has just so much
power, and no more. It is folly to talk about the Federal
Government running over, or absorbing the several State
Governments; the thing is absurd, and impossible. If it
ever could have done so, it was years ago, and is always
getting further from such the older we get.

On the other hand, the States can never encroach on
the Federal; because they operate on local affairs, the
domestic citizen, and are fully occupied in the same. All
this comes from actual statute.

Now, in regard to interests : I argue that no such disruption can occur; because a variety of interests, I think,
strengthens rather than weakens this bond. The North
needs the West and South to occupy her manufactories
and her ships. The West needs the North to supply her
with these elements of a market and transit; and she
needs the South to furnish an outlet for her products.
The South needs the North to manufacture her comforts,
and carry her millions away from the place of production,
most of which goes beyond the seas ; while she also needs
the breadstuffs of the West—not that the South could

not produce the same, but it is more profitable to produce something more valuable and exchange it. This I call the bond or "Union" of self-interest. Now, my fears about more territory does not really apply to territory in the abstract. It is the heterogeneous and mongrel races we get along with it which gives me alarm—not the soil, nor climate, nor country; but the character of the people we thus annex to us.

The great extent of country we have acquired by this war contains a class of people inimical to us in every respect, and yet they possess certain political rights which we may not deprive them of. They do not possess that intelligence which gives them a fair claim to civilisation, yet they are not fit subjects for the pupilage of the Indian or that of the negro. Hence it is that I fear their influence; superior civilisation of the Americans will gradually run over them, because they have not that protection of the negro, even, in the which conflicts will occur. However, I am not disposed to borrow trouble. As our Government was formed in reason, economy, and sound judgment, I am willing to trust to like elements to sustain it. It was, and is, an experiment; but has been so eminently successful that I cannot think it can fail, even on the score of self-interest. Besides all, I am a fatalist in Government. So are you; but the difference is, you hold to a fatality of destruction—I hold to a fatality of preservation. All apparent difficulties are at once buried into nothing with me when I come to reflect on the great heaving mass of Christianity, intelligence, and civilisation, of twenty millions of people, soon to be doubled and quadrupled. Your finely-drawn elements of "antagonism in races" sink to mere speculations. I do not say there may not be "innate differences" among classes of men, but I do say that all such must fade away before the moulding hand of time and true civilisation. And while all the present and future States of this nation are united by a written compact, for the purposes of a general national Government, so are they all united on even stronger grounds of continual advancement in Christianity, civilisation, and humanity. The South is Christianising the negroes, and benefits not only the negro in this work but millions in other lands receive almost an equal benefit in the negro's labour. The North receives full benefit from the same. The products of the negroes on this continent forms a wonderful element in the economy and habits of millions far distant from the place of production; while the negroes, in turn, are just so many consumers of Northern productions and aids to Northern commerce.

A small class of sickly sentimentalists in the North, and throughout the world, are striving to emancipate the bondsman more rapidly than he is fitted to receive it, but the great mass of intelligent people know that such a course is at once destructive to the best interest of the negro, and injures the whites, even thousands of miles distant from him. Hence, the idea is Utopian, and is on a par with your Northern spiritualism, short-lived at best, and not much while living.

Your want of faith, I think, comes from a failure to examine closely, first, the written Constitution; secondly, from a want of confidence in mankind; while I have not confidence in every man, yet, in the aggregate of man, I have the greatest faith.

Affectionately yours,

J. C. TURNLEY.

LETTER XXVII.

Kansas City, March 8, 1857.

Yours of last month chased me round for more than six hundred miles, but finally came safely to hand.

I had read the speech of Mr. Seward, which you refer to, with all the attention and close scrutiny which that man's sophistry requires, and it appears to my mind that I wrote you on the subject a few days after I read it. In this I may, perhaps, be mistaken; I hope, however, you slow coach people of Tennessee will not allow Mr. Seward's ventilation of his theories to disturb your quiet. That gentleman is one of the new lights, or "Latter-day Saints," in the political economy of America, and I had supposed you were all quite conversant with his revelations. For my own part, I have so long been reading his views and theories (none of which have ever yet proved half so true as those of Brigham Young on Mormonism), that I supposed every sensible man viewed Brigham, on religion, and Seward, on politics, about in the same light. There is one great difference, however—Brigham has not the power to do much harm, as his influence is confined to the few ignorant, deluded sensualists, who are lured to his flock more in search of freeholds, than any fixed knowledge of, or attachment to, that would-be Saint's religion; whereas Mr. Seward is the acknowledged prophet of all the Puritan and Democratic elements of the North-eastern States. His views, as expressed in his speeches respecting his " irrepressible conflict " between slave labour and free labour, is as false as it is cunning. It is Mr. Seward's mode, however, of still keeping under control, while he makes still hotter, the real antagonism of races which I have heretofore alluded to in my letters as existing

K

between the Northern and the Southern people. You do not tell me that Mr. Seward has one follower in Tennessee; in fact, I doubt whether he can have very many, even in the free States of the North-west. It would be strange, indeed, if Mr. Seward's theory could be believed, namely, that there is an irrepressible conflict between free labour of the North, and the slave labour of the South. Mr. Seward must know, and count largely on the ignorance and credulity of the people, to whom he makes this inflammatory remark. If such "irrepressible conflict" exists between slave labour of Tennessee, and the free labour of New York (this is what he says), why not a still greater conflict between that slave labour of Tennessee and the white labour of Tennessee? This latter every-body knows does not exist; hence, still less does the other exist. But millions of people in the North, to whom, and for whom Mr. Seward's views were uttered, will take for granted all he said, and will proceed accordingly. In fact, they have been, and are now proceeding on that assumption. No; the fact is, Mr. Seward himself don't believe that any such conflict exists, or ever has existed, but he only wants to try and create such conflict. His object is to try and produce that which he imagines might, ought, or should exist, and not that which he really thinks does, or ever has existed. In other words, Mr. Seward means to have a revolution, and if he can't get it in one way, he will in another; but, so far, his plan is to inoculate the mind of the Democratic masses in the North with his views and sentiments, so that he can lead them. When he has done this, then any action (how-ever revolutionary) will be supported by those masses. This is just now the theme, all over the North-eastern States; it is on the boards of every theatre; it is in the drama of that most infamous creature, "Mrs. H. B.

Stowe's book," two-thirds of which, by the bye, Mr. Seward himself wrote. This feeling of hatred is taught in every school and college; in every church it is preached Sunday and week-day. It were impossible for me, in a letter, to convey to you the perfect system of poisoning the ignorant masses in the North against the peace, the happiness, and domestic tranquillity of the Southern States. To see and know the whole, in all of its ramifications, its secret orders, and dark-lantern brotherhoods, would astonish you. All this exists, and will continue to exist; it will increase daily, until it culminates into revolution. This revolution was designed when Fremont was put forward by the Northern revolutionists, as candidate for President; his failure, however, delayed it, but the delay was not regretted by Mr. Seward and his partizan aids. By delay, they will gather strength; and nothing is truer than that this Northern Puritan revolutionary party design to prevent another national President of the United States.

It behoves the Southern States to look this matter squarely in the face; |not captiously and with bravado, and with an eye single to the protection of their slave property (although this is one of many causes they have to complain); but the entire South ought to come to some understanding, and every agricultural State act in harmony with a fixed plan of self-defence. For, I must here repeat what I have before said, which is, that the aim and drift of this revolutionary organisation all over the Puritan States is not alone, nor mainly, against slavery; but it is against everything and anything which supports and sustains the agricultural pursuits. Hence, you will ask me why is not this enmity directed also against the North-western States, which are also agricultural. My answer is, that it was for a time; but was withdrawn, seeing that the East relied on so many partisan leaders in Ohio, Indiana, and especially Illinois. They at once ceased everything like allusion to tariffs or agricultural interests, and determined to write on their flags and banners, "Down with negro slavery!" knowing that such labour is solely devoted to agriculture. After the Slave States are subdued, either by force, or by such legislation as will effectually place every tiller of the soil at the mercy of Eastern manufacturing task-masters and their co-workers, the commercial millionaires, their attention will be turned to the agricultural free States of the North-west. In fact, these North-western States people are of a very different kind of political economists from those of the South. Nearly all of the agriculturists are of comparative recent importation from foreign countries, who have been content in the Old World to cultivate but an acre of land; and they found themselves rich with the products of only ten acres. They are mostly of the Germans and Irish, who are quite content to till ten or twenty acres; and, as a general thing, they cultivate that amount of land much better than a man in Tennessee does his two hundred. Not only this; but they are very ignorant people, and the political partizan leaders of the North (of whom Mr. Seward is one of the most subtle and dangerous) are constantly drilling it into these German and Irish, Welsh, Danes, and Swedes, that the slave-owners of the South design to enslave them also! And it is a fact that many of these poor ignorant creatures really live in constant fear of this! Many of these new-comers to the West have been made to believe that negroes are white, and have been kidnapped by Southern people from the Northern States!

The fact is, you would be utterly astounded could you take a "peep in" behind the curtains, at all the infamous and diabolical machinery now in operation in the North-eastern and Western States to bring about a Revolution! Everything possible to conceive of is used for that purpose. Regularly paid agents are traversing the States north-west, to lecture to the people. Scarce a sermon is preached any more in a church, without at least half of it being a most terrific tirade against Southern people.

While passing through Rochester, New York, not long since, I had occasion to stop over Sunday, and attended a church called the "Congregationalists," and heard the dirtiest tirade imaginable! The church, or hall, was quite filled with men and women, all of the first people in that city. Their pious leader, after discoursing at great length on what God had assigned for him and his flock to do, closed out his "stock-in-trade" by telling them that the "Southern people were heathens," and had to be "Christianised!" "Not only this," said he, "but virtue and chastity are unknown among our Southern people, whether male or female!" This, I thought, was plain enough: when a preacher is piously listened to by the most respectable people in the town of Rochester, in the State of New York, while he asserts that the Christian agriculturists of neighbouring States are "heathens," "harlots," and "roués," I considered it time for me to leave; especially as my mother and sisters were included in the list!

I have alluded to this, as only one instance in ten thousand now going on in the North to poison the minds of the ignorant masses against the Southern States people. It is wide spread, and is having its effect. It must result in revolution. And Mr. Seward, and his aids and assistants, are aiming at this. The South, in the meanwhile, do not suspect what is going on. True, the South talk much about being compelled to secede from the

Union, in order to secure their rights, &c.; but this is just what the Northern leaders want; because then will they have succeeded in their aim for revolution; and out of that revolution will hope to obtain better results and greater benefits for the Puritans than they did out of that of 1776, which they inaugurated for the same selfish purposes.

Affectionately yours,

PARMENAS.

LETTER XXVIII.

Salt Lake City, July 25th, 1860.

MY DEAR SISTER,

In my last letter I alluded to the cause of the present political differences extant in our country. I gave you my views of what I conceive to be the true cause—differing, very much, from the generally-received opinion that it is slavery. I showed that the cause of disagreement is inherent in the different classes of human beings composing our country. I feel sure that, on due reflection, your mind will feel the force of my argument, and you will not fail to perceive, in addition, the ten thousand evidences, daily offered to one's view, that this deep-set antagonism is not to be ignored nor overlooked, even temporarily, merely on the announcement in the halls of Congress, on the stump, or in the pulpit, that " we are all one, " we are brothers, sisters," &c., &c.

Neither is it necessary for you nor I to pass sentence on either of the classes, or decide which is right, and which wrong. This would be, at once, attaching ourselves to one or the other class, and very soon thus become incapable of discussing either with freedom or unbiased feeling.

At the same time, the fact is true, that nature has undoubtedly assigned us to one or the other of the numerous classes or casts; or, if you please, "types" of the human family; and it would be folly to attempt to separate ourselves from that class, whether we are conscious of the fact or not.

But I omit much that might be said on this subject, and come at once to your second question, viz.: "What is to be the ultimate result of this difference or disagreement?" I cannot conceive that any different results can follow in our own country, than such as have always followed disagreements among the various types or casts of mankind. It is not man's nature to be either charitable or peaceable. The reverse is rather true. Man is by nature oppressive and warlike in his proclivities. These traits of man's nature may be trained and directed and moulded into this or that shape, and greatly modified for a long series of years, even for centuries; but the element is still there, and ultimately it breaks forth and shows itself in every manner of hostility and revenge that human skill is capable of inventing.

Now, when we come to examine the history of men from all known sources—as well profane as what we call inspired—we find that differences and dissensions are coeval with their very beginning on earth. But, there does not appear, in any period, or among any people, but one cause or element of disturbance. However numerous the causes appear to be, yet all are consequents of one first cause. It is customary for us in our present day to speak of the unsettled condition of society in different States, nations, &c. We see at the present moment what we call a useless and unstable state of mind among the people of France, England, Austria, and other provinces, and we all ascribe to this disaffection political causes.

This is as erroneous as to say the slavery question is the cause of our own troubles.

Civil Government, old as it is, is yet the second condition in which mankind have tried to live in harmony. Nearly every form of civil government possible to conceive of has been tried; yet, not one form was ever devised or practised that did not include in its operations, its ramifications and effects, all known ideas of an existence after this life. The three hundred and twenty different beliefs among tribes on earth, as to the existence of their souls and bodies after this life, enter into every attempt at social civil government! Now, the framers of our social system endeavoured to establish a Government free from all sects, creeds, and belief; yet, so far from doing it, we see they have included all; and the United States is the field of battle for the votaries of a hundred religious creeds to fight the battle of faith. They are all drilling their recruits, and have been for two hundred years.

It is this inherent element which induces or solicits different religious beliefs, that I allude to as being irreconcilable. Hence, it follows that only those creatures, whose belief and faith are similar, can possibly cohere for a length of time in one social compact. This, too, brings me to the point, which I have before had occasion to speak of, which is, that preachers are the agents throughout the world of strife, dissension, blood, and desolation! They are the recruiting officers of hostile sentiments, the drill sergeants of squads, and the commanders of the thousands on the bloody fields of battle. But, we know of no period of the world in which they have not existed—and always filling the offices, too, in which I have assigned them. The inference is, therefore, that they were designed by the Author of all things either as a curse or a blessing,— we know not which.

The sentiment of hostility, therefore, between our different sections of country is more a religious difference than anything else; and, hence, it is simply idle to expect a cessation until the hundreds of thousands on both sides shall have been offered as a sacrifice to their respective angry Gods. This conflict may be hastened or delayed a little, but not wholly averted by any means. Individuals as well as communities always make false attacks. If one religious sect wants to supplant or make war on another, it assumes at once part of the dress of its intended victim. This is necessary in order to create division—division being essential to success. Hence, we find old school and new school Presbyterians, North Methodists and South Methodists, North Baptists and South Baptists, Roman Catholics and Holy Catholics, &c., &c. Likewise, in political communities, the professed object is never the real one.

Now, to apply this course of reasoning, and this species of action, to the disaffected parties in the United States, is plain and easy; as likewise to discover the falsity of design, that one class of people want to see all others free, &c., &c., while another desires to have a portion subject unto them. Now, the latter is evidently in accordance with the instincts of mankind. We all know that if we have one trait more marked than another in our very nature, it is the desire to have the control of others, and to have them entirely subject unto us. This' is true in practice and in theory with every human being that was ever born on earth. God requires subjection unto him, Christ desired subjection unto himself—he in turn being subject unto the Father. The Apostles and Prophets desired submission unto them, while they were lesser than Christ, &c.

In all classes and grades of society, not one being but

covets power and control over others; so, likewise, since the world began, has this power of one over another been exercised. One human creature has owned and used and bartered and sold another at pleasure for his own benefit. At one period, the vanquished tribes in battle were the willing chattels of their conquerors. Later in history, persons taken in battle were transferable chattels; and well-defined rules of service and transfer were laid down and practised three thousand years ago. This subserviency of one class to another is as universal over the world to-day, as it ever was? and it will always continue to exist.

The masters and the servants or slaves shift and change with the restless changes in all human affairs. The strife is continuous, and is, and always will be, a war of races. In some countries there is white slavery, in others black slavery. One set of rules govern the service at one place, and another set of rules at another place.— Might rules always, whatever we may think of right or wrong. The very opposition now rampant in one section against African slavery, is the measure of the intensity of the human heart in favour of white slavery. The stronger will be the victor.

The war of one class on another, is the result of frequent and easy intercourse. We are told among individuals, that "too much familiarity breeds contempt." Not less true is the adage when applied to States or nations. The difficulties among European nations is in direct ratio of their increased commercial and other intimate relations. Those nations most exclusive and retired —Japan and China for example—are least changeable and fluctuating in government and society. Sectional troubles in the United States have increased directly in proportion to the facilities of frequent and ready intercourse. An union of the several States was of doubtful propriety in the first place, was viewed with distrust by many, and absolutely opposed by some of the wisest heads of that day.

Even that union, when consummated, was differently construed and understood by the contracting parties; one claiming it to be a kind of "alliance offensive and defensive" only; while the other maintained that it was a consolidation. Whether meant to be the latter or not, we see it has practically proved to be such. The rights and privileges claimed by States, for example, we see is merely a nominal, not a practical power. Whether "might makes right" or not, we constantly see that might is having its own course. Might is forcing a sameness in all society. It is mixing up heterogeneous elements under guise of moulding all into one mass, which we know from experience cannot be done peaceably; but that the continued attempts must bring its fruits, which are revolution, strife, blood, anarchy, and, lastly, peace, with the separate classes of the "ruler" and the "ruled," or the "masters" and the "slaves." It is merely a turn of the wheel of society on the same old axis.

But my hour has expired. I must hasten to a close; and, I think, I have answered your second question. Revolution between North and South is inevitable. It must come. Every pulsation of the human heart tends to its speedy commencement. It may be one, two, five, or even ten years. But come it must and will. Neither is it to be dreaded, as some think. On the contrary, it is as necessary as a thunder-storm is to cool and purify the infected atmosphere. There is a grandeur and a sublimity in the consequences to follow such a conflict, as fills the heart with the greatest ambition. The Northern hordes, although composed of many types of the human species—

and therefore, quite dissimilar—are yet an unit on the subject of this warfare; and as an unit, they fully enjoy the sublimity and magnificence of the engagement. Let the Southern people feel likewise. Let them prepare for it, and, instead of being any longer the conservators of a dis-united Union, let them, as an unit, sever the cable, and the ship will float free and easy, ready for the fight.

The best mode of doing this is comprised in your third question; and I will answer you on that point the first leisure hour.

The pang of death, which was the "union in sentiment," has already been felt; and has expanded itself in words and threats. The practical consummation of the separation, for the first few years to come, will be merely political financiering.

" The " platform " or " declaration," set forth by the Convention which has lately nominated Mr. A. Lincoln (at Chicago, Illinois) as their candidate for the next President, is a clear and emphatic "declaration of war against the Constitution of the United States!" It cannot be interpreted in any other light. In fact, such are its words and resolves from beginning to the end. Surely no honest lover of Government under the American Constitution can for a moment entertain the idea of casting his vote on the side of such a declaration of war! Let the Southern States accept this declaration of war by the Puritans—not with sword in hand, but by quietly withdrawing from a Union which has ceased to exist. An alliance, by the South, immediately with all Christian nations of Europe will further tend to avert blood, at least till she shall have time to be the better prepared. Let the South throw open her ports to foreign nations and the remaining States.

Now, in order for the Southern mind to arrive at this

course of procedure, they must cease brooding over the "point of attack," pointed at by their Northern enemies, which is slavery. As I have before said, this is a "feint" on the part of the Northern Generals. They are not intending to attack slavery. The North may not especially *crave black slaves*, but they are more wedded *to slavery in the abstract* than any other people, and would no more give up slavery than they would their lives.

In fact, a system of "indentured" service among whites—which is slavery under another name—must, from the existing state of society in the North, be put into a more extensive and a more practical shape in a very short time. The "poor-houses," "alms-houses," "houses of correction," and last, not least, the "insane asylums," must all very soon be merged into a system of slavery, by which the poor and needy, the wayward and perverse, shall be supplied and kept in subjection. The insanity, too, in six cases out of eight, results from a destitution, and an utter inability to self-government and self-control.

Just think of one State alone having two hundred thousand of destitute poor! and, at the same time, twenty-seven thousand of insane! making a total of two hundred and twenty-seven thousand of inferior creatures demanding a state of servitude! Voluntary contributions will do very well to talk about, but not be practised to a great extent. The remedy—the only remedy, is in the entire transfer of the body, the time, the intellect of the inferior to the superior. Nowhere do you find such insanity among slaves, whether black or white.

But want of time bids we close for the present.

Your brother,

PARMENAS.

APPENDIX.

THE following very pertinent and truthful remarks we find in the *North Western Church*, of February 15, 1863. As it is a little piece of history, touching Puritans, we append it to what has been said concerning them in the foregoing letters :—

" Mr. Editor,—These are inquiring times ; men are searching, on all hands, for solutions to many questions that were once supposed settled. A great many hoary old shams that have imposed on them are getting rapidly pitched into the gutter. A great many things they had supposed true are turning out false. The thing must go on. I design doing my small share, then, to help.

" The Americans have a certain distinct type of national character. We have certain clearly-defined national ideas. Where do we get them ? Last month, on 'Forefather's day,' a thousand voices answered, ' We got them all from Plymouth Rock. They all came over in the ' Mayflower.' A noble band of pilgrims fleeing from persecution in wicked old Europe, came over to the desert New World, and established here freedom to worship God, free schools, free presses, universal suffrage, and every noble thing there is in America.'

" That was the answer at all the ' pilgrim dinners ' in December. It is also the answer in half our school readers, and so-called school histories. The innocent children of all Americans are taught that they, poor little things, are descended from ' our forefathers' of the ' Mayflower ;' that all the people of this broad continent came from the loins of the Rev. Mr. Robinson and his congregation ; that the gentlemen in steeple-crowned hats, in short, made America.

" Let us look at it. In the first place, then, the Puritan emigration was but a drop in the bucket; it formed scarcely the hundredth part of the original emigration. It was not the first emigration, either. Flourishing colonies were planted years before in various parts of the country. There were English in Virginia; Swedes and Fins coming into New Jersey; Dutch in New York; French Huguenots into Carolina. As near as I can make out, the proportion of people now in the United States of English descent is about six millions; of these, about two millions are of Puritan descent.

" Now, what did the Puritans come to America for? Mrs. Hemans says, to establish ' freedom to worship God.' Mr. Beecher, *et id omne genus*, says, to establish this, and escape persecution. What does history say? They came simply to better their condition. They emigrated from precisely the motive that caused emigration then, and causes it now, and ever will cause it—the prospect of larger material benefits. They emigrated from Holland, not from England. They certainly were not persecuted in Holland. I deny that they were persecuted in England; at all events, they were not troubled on account of their religion, in Holland. Europe did not drive them out. They were doing well among the Dutch. But mark the Puritans. ' It grieved their hearts that the Dutch would not reform their church according to the pure word of God.' They left Holland because they could not compel the Dutch to turn Puritans. That is their own word. Well, in 1620, being then in Leyden, and being satisfied they couldn't turn Dutchmen into Puritans, they concluded to leave, and asked James I. for a grant of land. James, an Episcopal king, gave them a grant, the exclusive right to the soil, to the fisheries, and to the trade. That, certainly, is not persecution.

"They came for the land, the fisheries, and the trade; and we find, as a specimen of Puritan gratitude, that the first row they got into was a fight with their old hosts the Dutch, because they trespassed on these same fisheries.

"Now, what did they bring, and what did they leave? Separation of Church and State? Edward Everett, a very fine talker, says yes. Judge Story, a man of more brains, and less fine writing, says: 'The fundamental error of our ancestors, an error which began with their settlement of this colony (Massachusetts), was a doctrine which has been happily exploded, I mean the necessity of a union of Church and State. To this they clung, as to their ark of safety. In fact, tithes were abolished finally in Massachusetts in 1834.'

"Toleration is an American idea. Did they leave us that? Did they bring that ' Freedom to worship God?' In 1658 they cut off the ears of three Quakers. In 1659 they hung a dozen or so, and would not allow their friends to bury them. In 1660 they 'suspended' a few more; a poor old woman, who had to be carried to the gallows, among the rest. Even in 1739 they 'drummed' Mr. Finlay, a distinguished Presbyterian divine, out of the colony. They hanged Roman Catholics. They cut the tongues out of Quakers. They whipped Presbyterians. They fined a man for using the Episcopal Prayer-book. All this is matter of history.

"But the reply is, ' This was the fault of the times.' Of course, then, the argument is given up. They were really no better than the wicked, these pious Puritans. But it was not the fault of the times. They were behind the times. They persecuted after all the world ceased to persecute. They were hanging and slitting tongues for fifty years, against the world's remonstrances. The last death for religion in Old England took place in 1612, before the landing on Plymouth Rock. In 1660, forty-eight years after, the Puritans were hanging Quakers in New England. Before they left Europe, death for religion had ceased; Europe had given up fire and faggot, and these delightful Puritans came hither, and revived and stuck to the cast-off barbarities of the Old World. In 1720, in Massachusetts, they enacted a law of death against a Roman Catholic. In 1774, they sent a formal protest against the ' Quebec Act,' by which the British Parliament tolerated that religion in Canada. In England, if a man absented himself from public worship, he was fined one shilling; in Massachusetts he was fined five; and in Plymouth, where the ' Rock' is, he was fined ten. For non-conformity to established Congregationalism, the fine was forty shillings a month, and if the men were ' incorrigible,' the law said death. The people of England remonstrated—even Puritans in England. Vane remonstrated. Salstonstall remonstrated; ' These rigid ways have laid you low in the hearts of the faithful in England.' Mark the answer, thoroughly Puritan, ' God forbid our love for truth should grow so cold that we should tolerate such errors.' ' In this persecuting policy,' says Judge Story, ' our ancestors persevered against every remonstrance at home and abroad.' Their own words are, ' Toleration is a sin in rulers.' The facts of history are, that the Puritans of New England persecuted when the world was crying out in horror; that they defended their bitter bigotry and narrow bloodthirsty intolerance when the whole civilized world had dropped persecution for opinion's sake in shame. Cotton Mather wrote the last words that were ever written in the English tongue in defence of religious persecution. The last blood shed by Saxon hands for religion's sake they shed, one hundred years after England had dropped that devil's work for

L

ever. And the only blood ever shed on this continent for religion's sake was shed in Plymouth and Massachusetts colonies. It is time that fact was distinctly known.

"The Roman Catholics in Maryland, the Episcopalians in Virginia, the Quakers in Pennsylvania, the Dutch in New York, did establish and practice 'liberty of conscience,' but never the Puritans of New England. The bitterest fault they ever found with Charles II. was that he interfered, by royal pardon, to save from the stake some Anabaptists whom the Puritans were bound to burn. That, in their eyes, was the crime of his life. They tolerate! Why, Story says that in 1676 five-sixths of all the inhabitants of Massachusetts were disfranchised, not to be tried as freemen, or have freemen's rights, because the law of that colony required every voter to be a Congregationalist!

"I have examined historically those two points, and there is the result. To the Puritans we do not owe our toleration, nor our separation of Church and State. I am not aware that we owe them any of our American ideas. The only presses gagged on this continent Puritans gagged. The most restricted suffrage exercised was in Puritan Massachusetts. The narrowest and most illiberal repression of opinion has been there. They, and only they, came to this country with ideas which our American life has swept utterly away. The notions every American condemns, the practices every American instinctively abhors, are all Puritan notions and Puritan practices, and came over in the 'Mayflower.'"

I am compelled to leave out of this little volume many letters which I had hoped to be able to insert; but it was not in my power to obtain the manuscript, because hostile and contending armies cut off all intercourse with the persons who have the originals.

For the same reason I am compelled to leave out the interesting description of Mormons and Mormonism, which is mentioned in one of the preceding letters. I regret this, also, because the writer gives a most clear demonstration of the fact that Puritanism is also the foundation of Mormonism. Truly is this one of those cases, not rare in the world, where the extremes of fanaticism meet!

I will close this book, however, with extracts from the late speech, in Congress, of that most profound statesman and Christian patriot, the Hon. C. L. Vallandigham, of Ohio, on the condition of the American nation, delivered before the House on the 14th January, 1863. History hath already recorded it, and it will be read by millions yet unborn, whose voices will one day be raised to execrate and denounce the most infamous fiends that ever acquired office of trust only to destroy the same, and who now sit in state at Washington city, exulting in the ruin, blood, and carnage which they, and they alone, have produced. It will be recollected that a couple of months before Mr. Vallandigham made this speech, elections had taken place throughout the Western States—Ohio among others, —in which that gentleman had been endorsed by his constituents by heavy majorities, and in all other States, the popular vote had been most condemnatory of the Executive and his Cabinet.

It is on this account that one dare to deliver the following speech. No doubt exists but that fear of the populace caused the Executive and his Cabinet to let pass in silence Mr. Vallandigham's most truthful remarks.

*The State of the Union.—Speech of C. L. Vallandigham,
of Ohio, delivered in the United States House of
Representatives, January 14th, 1863.*

Mr. VALLANDIGHAM. Indorsed at the recent election
within the same district for which I still hold a seat on this
floor, by a majority four times greater than ever before, I
speak to-day in the name and by the authority of the
people, who, for six years, have intrusted me with the
office of a Representative. Loyal, in the true and highest
sense of the word, to the Constitution and the Union,
they have proved themselves devotedly attached to, and
worthy of, the liberties to secure which the Union and the
Constitution were established. With candor and freedom,
therefore, as their representative, and with much plainness
of speech, but with the dignity and decency due to this
presence, I propose to consider the state of the Union to-
day, and to inquire what the duty is of every public man,
and every citizen, in this the very crisis of the Great
Revolution.

It is now two years, sir, since Congress assembled
soon after the Presidential election. A sectional anti-
slavery party had just succeeded, through the forms of the
Constitution. For the first time a President had been
chosen upon a platform of avowed hostility to an institution peculiar to nearly one-half of the States of the Union,
and who had himself proclaimed that there was an irrepressible conflict because of that institution between the
States; and that the Union could not endure "part slaves
and part free." Congress met, therefore, in the midst of
the profoundest agitation, not here only, but throughout
the entire South. Revolution glared upon us. Repeated
efforts for conciliation and compromise were attempted in
Congress and out of it. All were rejected by the party

just coming into power, except only the promise in the last hour of the session, and that, too, against the consent of a majority of that party, both in the Senate and House— that Congress (not the executive) should never be authorised to abolish or interfere with slavery in the States where it existed. South Carolina seceded; Georgia, Alabama, Florida, Mississippi, Louisiana, and Texas speedily followed. The Confederate Government was established. The other slave States held back. Virginia demanded a peace congress—the commissioners met, and, after some time, agreed upon terms of final adjustment; but, neither in the Senate nor the House, were they allowed even a respectful consideration. The President elect left his home in February, and journeyed towards this capital, jesting as he came, proclaiming that the crisis was only artificial, and that "nobody was hurt." He entered this city under cover of night, and in disguise. On the 4th of March he was inaugurated, surrounded by soldiery; and, swearing to support the Constitution of the United States, announced in the same breath that the platform of his party should be the law unto him. From that moment all hope of peaceable adjustment fled. But for a little while, either with unsteadfast sincerity, or in premeditated deceit, the policy of peace was proclaimed, even to the evacuation of Sumpter and the other Federal forts and arsenals in the seceded States. Why that policy was suddenly abandoned, time will fully disclose. But, just after the Spring elections, and the secret meeting in this city of the Governors of the several Northern and Western States, a fleet of —— vessels, carrying —— men, was sent down ostensibly to provision Fort Sumpter. The authorities of South Carolina eagerly accepted the challenge, and bombarded the fort into surrender, while the fleet fired not a gun; but, just so soon as the flag was struck, bore away

and returned to the North. It was Sunday, the 14th day
of April, 1861; and that day the President, in fatal
haste, and without the advice or consent of Congress,
issued his proclamation, dated the next day, calling out
seventy-five thousand militia for three months, to re-possess
the forts, places, and property seized from the United
States, and commanding the insurgents to disperse in
twenty days. Again the gauge was taken up by the South,
and thus the flames of a civil war, the grandest, bloodiest,
and saddest in history, lighted up the whole heavens.
Virginia forthwith seceded; North Carolina, Tennessee,
and Arkansas followed; Delaware, Maryland, Kentucky,
and Missouri were in a blaze of agitation, and, within a
week from the proclamation, the line of the Confederate
States was transferred from the cotton States to the
Potomac, and almost to the Ohio and the Missouri, and
their population and fighting men doubled.

In the North and West, too, the storm raged with the
fury of a hurricane. Never in history was anything equal
to it. Men, women, and children, native and foreign
born, Church and State, clergy and laymen, were all swept
along with the current. Distinction of age, sex, station,
party, perished in an instant. Thousands bent before the
tempest; and here and there only was one found bold
enough—fool-hardy enough, it may have been—to bend
not, and upon him it fell as a consuming fire. The spirit
of persecution for opinion's sake, almost extinct in the
Old World, now, by some mysterious transmigration,
appeared incarnate in the New. Social relations were
dissolved; friendships broken up; the ties of family and
kindred snapped asunder. Stripes and hanging were
everywhere threatened, sometimes executed. Assassi-
nation was invoked ; slander sharpened his tooth; falsehood crushed truth to the earth ; reason fled ; madness

reigned, Not justice only escaped to the skies; but peace returned to the bosom of God, whence she came. The gospel of love perished; hate sat enthroned, and the sacrifices of blood smoked upon every altar.

But the reign of the mob was inaugurated only to be supplanted by the iron domination of arbitrary power. Constitutional limitation was broken down; *habeas corpus* fell; liberty of the press, of speech, of the person, of mails, of travel, of one's own house, and of religion; the right to bear arms, due process of law, judicial trial, trial by jury, trial at all; every badge and muniment of freedom in republican government or kingly government — all went down at a blow; the chief law officer of the Crown —I beg pardon, sir, but it is easy to fall into this courtly language—the Attorney-General, first of all men, proclaimed in the United States the maxim of Roman servility: Whatever pleases the President, that is law! Prisoners of State were then first heard of here. Midnight and arbitrary arrests commenced; travel was interdicted; trade embargoed; passports demanded; Bastiles were introduced; strange oaths invented; a secret police organised; "piping" began; informers multiplied; spies now first appeared in America. The right to declare war, to raise and support armies, and to provide and maintain a navy was usurped by the Executive; and in a little more than two months a land and naval force of over three hundred thousand men was in the field or upon the sea. An army of public plunderers followed, and corruption struggled with power in friendly strife for the mastery at home.

On 4th of July, Congress met: not to seek peace; not to rebuke usurpation nor to restrain power; not certainly to deliberate; not even to legislate, but to register and ratify the edicts and acts of the Executive;

and in your language, sir, upon the first day of the session, to invoke an universal baptism of fire and blood amid the roar of cannon and the din of battle. Free speech was had only at the risk of a prison, possibly of life. Opposition was silenced by the fierce clamour of "disloyalty." All business not of war was voted out of order. Five hundred thousand men, an immense navy, and two hundred and fifty millions of money, were speedily granted. In twenty, at most int sixy days, the rebellion was to be crushed out. To doubt it was treason. Abject submission was demanded.   Lay down your arms, sue for peace, surrender your leader—forfeiture, death—this was the only language heard on this floor. The galleries responded; the corridors echoed; and contractors, and placemen, and other venal patriots everywhere gnashed upon the friends of peace as they passed by. In five weeks seventy-eight public and private acts and joint resolutions, with declaratory resolutions, in the Senate and House, quite as numerous, all full of slaughter, were hurried through without delay and almost without debate.

Thus was civil war inaugurated in America. Can any man to-day see the end of it?

And now pardon me, sir, if I pause here a moment to define my own position at this time upon this great question.

Sir, I am one of that number who have opposed abolitionism, or the political development of the anti-slavery sentiment of the North and West, from the beginning. In school, at college, at the bar, in public assemblies, in the Legislature, in Congress, boy and man, as a private citizen and in public life, in time of peace and in time of war, at all times and at every sacrifice, I have fought against it. It cost me ten years' exclusion from office and honour, at that period of life when honours are sweetest. No

matter : I learned early to do right and wait.   Sir, it is but
the development of the spirit of intermeddling, whose
children are strife and murder.   Cain troubled himself
about the sacrifice of Abel, and slew him.   Most of the
wars and contentions, and litigation and bloodshed, from
the beginning of time, have been its fruits.   The spirit of
non-intervention is the very spirit of peace and concord.
I do not believe that if slavery had never existed here we
would have had no sectional controversies.   This very
civil war might have happened fifty, perhaps a hundred
years later.   Other and stronger causes of discontent and
of disunion, it may be, have existed between other States
and sections, and are now being developed every day into
maturity.   The spirit of intervention assumed the form
of abolitionism because slavery was odious in name and
by association to the Northern mind, and because it was
that which most obviously marks the different civilisations
of the two sections.   The South herself, in her early and
later efforts to rid herself of it, had exposed the weak and
offensive parts of slavery to the world.   Abolition intermeddling taught her at last to search for and defend the
assumed social, economic, and political merit and value of
the institution.   But there never was an hour from the
beginning when it did not seem to me as clear as the sun
at broad noon, that the agitation in any form in the North
and West of the slavery question must sooner or later end
in disunion and civil war.   This was the opinion and pre-
diction for years of Whig and Democratic statesmen alike ;
and after the unfortunate dissolution of the Whig Party
in 1854, and the organisation of the present Republican
party upon an exclusively anti-slavery and sectional basis,
the event was inevitable; because, in the then existing
temper of the public mind, and after the education
through the press and by the pulpit, the lecture, and the

political canvass for twenty years, of a generation taught to hate slavery and the South, the success of that party, possessed, as it was, of every engine of political, business, social, and religious influence, was certain. It was only a question of time, and short time. Such was its strength, indeed, that I do not believe that the union of the Democratic Party in 1860 on any candidate, even though he had been supported also by an entire so-called Conservative or anti-Lincoln vote of the country, would have availed to defeat it; and if it had, the success of the abolition party would only have been postponed four years longer. The disease had fastened too strongly upon the system to be healed until it had run its course. The doctrine of the " irrepressible conflict " had been taught too long, and accepted too widely and earnestly to die out, until it should culminate in secession and disunion; and, if coercion were resorted to, then in civil war. I believed from the first that it was the purpose of some of the apostles of that doctrine to force a collision between the North and the South, either to bring about a separation or to find a vain but bloody pretext for abolishing slavery in the States. In any event, I knew, or thought I knew, that the end was certain collision and death to the Union.

*　　*　　*　　*　　*　　*

Believing thus, I have for years past denounced those who taught that doctrine with all the vehemence, the bitterness, if you choose—I thought it a righteous, a patriotic bitterness—of an earnest and impassioned nature. Thinking thus, I forewarned all who believed the doctrine, or followed the party which taught it, with a sincerity and a depth of conviction as profound as ever penetrated the heart of man. And when, for eight years past, over and over again, I have proclaimed to the people that the suc-

cess of a sectional anti-slavery party would be the beginning of disunion and civil war in America, I believed it.
I did. I had read history, and studied human nature, and
meditated for years upon the character of our institutions
and form of government, and of the people South as well
as North; and I could not doubt the event. But the
people did not believe me, nor those older and wiser and
greater than I. They rejected the prophecy, and stoned
the prophets. The candidate of the republican party was
chosen President. Secession began. Civil war was imminent. It was no petty insurrection; no temporary combi-
nation to obstruct the execution of the laws in certain
States; but a Revolution, systematic, deliberate, determined, and with the consent of a majority of the people
of each State which seceded. Causeless it may have been;
wicked it may have been; but there it was; not to be
railed at, still less to be laughed at, but to be dealt with
by statesmen as a fact. No display of vigour or force
alone, however sudden or great, could have arrested it
even at the outset. It was disunion at last. The wolf
had come. But civil war had not yet followed. In my
deliberate and most solemn judgment, there was but one
wise and masterly mode of dealing with it. Non-coercion
would avert civil war, and compromise crush out both
abolitionism and secession. The parent and the child
would thus both perish. But a resort to force would at
once precipitate a war, hasten secession, extend disunion,
and, while it lasted, utterly cut off all hope of compromise.
I believed that war, if long enough continued, would be
final, eternal disunion. I said it: I meant it; and, accordingly, to the utmost of my ability and influence, I exerted
myself in behalf of the policy of non-coercion. It was
adopted by Mr. Buchanan's administration, with the

almost unanimous consent of the Democratic and Constitutional Union parties in and out of Congress; and, in February, with a concurrence of a majority of the Republican party in the Senate and this House. But that party, most disastrously for the country, refused all compromise. How, indeed, could they accept any? That which the South demanded and the Democratic and Conservative parties of the North and West were willing to grant, and which alone could avail to keep the peace and save the Union, implied a surrender of the sole vital element of the party and its platform—of the very principle, in fact, upon which it had just won the contest for the Presidency; not, indeed, by a majority of the popular vote—the majority was nearly a million against it—but under the form of the Constitution. Sir, the crime, the "high crime" of the Republican party was not so much its refusal to compromise, as its original organisation upon a basis and doctrine wholly inconsistent with the stability of the constitution and the peace of the Union.

But to resume: The session of Congress expired. The President elect was inaugurated; and now, if only the policy of non-coercion could be maintained, and war thus averted, time would do its work in the North and the South, and final peaceable adjustment and reunion be secured. Some time in March it was announced that the President had resolved to continue the policy of his predecessor, and even go a step further, and evacuate Sumpter and the other Federal forts and arsenals in the seceded States. His own party acquiesced; the whole country rejoiced. The policy of non-coercion had triumphed, and, for once, sir, in my life, I found myself in an immense majority. No man then pretended that a Union founded in consent could be cemented by force.

Nay, more, the President and the Secretary of State went further. Said Mr. Seward, in an official diplomatic letter to Mr. Adams:

"For these reasons he [the President] would not be disposed to reject a cardinal dogma of theirs [the secessionists], namely, that the Federal Government could not reduce the seceding States to obedience by conquest, although he were disposed to question that proposition. But in fact the President willingly accepts it as true. Only an imperial or despotic Government could subjugate thoroughly disaffected and insurrectionary members of the State."

Pardon me, sir, but I beg to know whether this conviction of the President and his Secretary is not the philosophy of the persistent and most vigorous efforts made by this administration, and first of all through this same Secretary, the moment war broke out and ever since till the late elections, to convert the United States into an imperial or despotic Government? But Mr. Seward adds, and I agree with him:

"'This Federal republican system of ours is, of all forms of Government, the very one which is most unfitted for such a labour."

This, sir, was on the 10th of April, and yet that very day the fleet was under sail for Charleston. The policy of peace had been abandoned. Collision followed; the militia was ordered out; civil war began.

Now, sir, on the 14th of April I believed that coercion would bring on war, and war disunion. More than that, I believed, what you all in your hearts believe to-day, that the South could never be conquered—never. And not that only, but I was satisfied—and you of the Abolition party have now proved it to the world—that the secret but real purpose of the war was to abolish slavery in the States. In any event, I did not doubt that whatever

might be the momentary impulses of those in power, and
whatever pledges they might make in the midst of the
fury for the Constitution, the Union, and the flag, yet the
natural and inexorable logic of revolutions would, sooner
or later, drive them into that policy, and with it to its final
but inevitable result, the change of our present demo-
cratical form of Government into an Imperial despotism.

These were my convictions on the 14th of April. Had
I changed them on the 15th, when I read the President's
Proclamation, and become convinced that I had been
wrong all my life, and that all history was a fable, and all
human nature false in its development from the beginning
of time, I would have changed my public conduct also.
But my convictions did not change. I thought that, if
war was disunion on the 14th of April, it was equally disunion on the 15th, and at all times. Believing this, I
could not, as an honest man, a Union man, and a patriot,
lend an active support to the war; and I did not. I had
rather my right arm were plucked from its socket and cast
into eternal burnings, than, with my convictions, to have
thus defiled my soul with the guilt of moral perjury. Sir,
I was not taught in that school which proclaims that "all
is fair in politics." I loathe, abhor, and detest the exe-
crable maxim. I stamp upon it. No State can endure a
single generation whose public men practise it. Whoever
teaches it is a corrupter of youth. What we most want in
these times, and at all times, is honest and independent
public men. That man who is dishonest in politics is not
honest, at heart, in anything; and sometimes moral
cowardice is dishonesty. Do right; and trust to God, and
truth, and the people. Perish office, perish honour, perish
life itself; but do the thing that is right, and do it like a
man. I did it. Certainly, sir, I could not doubt what he
must suffer who dare defy the opinions and the passions,

not to say the madness, of twenty million people. Had I
not read history? Did I not know human nature? But
I appealed to time, and right nobly hath the avenger
answered me.

I did not support the war; and to-day I bless God
that not the smell of so much as one drop of its blood is
upon my garments. Sir, I censure no brave man who
rushed patriotically into this war; neither will I quarrel
with any one, here or elsewhere, who gave it an honest
support. Had their convictions been mine, I, too, would
doubtless have done as they did. With my convictions I
could not. But I was a Representative. War existed—
by whose act no matter—not mine. The President, the
Senate, the House, and the country, all said that there
should be war—war for the Union; a union of consent
and goodwill. Our Southern brethren were to be whipped
back into love and fellowship at the point of the bayonet.
Oh, monstrous delusion! I can comprehend a war to compel
people to accept a master; to change a form of Government;
to give up territory; to abolish a domestic institution—
in short, a war of conquest and subjugation; but a war for
Union. Was the Union thus made? Was it ever thus
preserved? Sir, history will record that after nearly six
thousand years of folly and wickedness in every form and
administration of Government, theocratic, democratic,
monarchic, olicharchic, despotic, and mixed, it was reserved
to American statesmanship in the nineteenth century of
the Christian era to try the grand experiment on a scale
the most costly and gigantic in its proportions, of creating
love by force, and developing fraternal affection by war;
and history will record, too, on the same page, the utter,
disastrous, and most bloody failure of the experiment.

But to return : the country was at war; and I belonged
to that school of politics which teaches that when we are

at war, the Government—I do not mean the Executive alone, but the Government—is entitled to demand and have, without resistance, such number of men, and such amount of money and supplies generally, as may be necessary for the war, until an appeal can be had to the people. Before that tribunal alone, in the first instance, must the question of the continuance of the war be tried. This was Mr. Calhoun's opinion, and he laid it down very broadly and strongly in a speech on the Loan Bill, in 1841. Speaking of supplies, he said:

"I hold that there is a distinction in this respect between a state of peace and war. In the latter, the right of withholding supplies ought ever to be held subordinate to the energetic and successful prosecution of the war. I go further, and regard the withholding supplies, with a view of forcing the country into a dishonourable peace, as not only to be, what it has been called, moral treason, but very little short of actual treason itself."

Upon this principle, sir, he acted afterwards in the Mexican war. Speaking of that war in 1847, he said:

"Every senator knows that I was opposed to the war; but none knows but myself the depth of that opposition. With my conception of its character and consequences, it was impossible for me to vote for it."

And again, in 1848:

"But, after war was declared, by authority of the Government, I acquiesced in what I could not prevent, and which it was impossible for me to arrest; and I then felt it to be my duty to limit my efforts to give such direction to the war as would, as far as possible, prevent the evils and dangers with which it threatened the country and its institutions."

Sir, I adopt all this as my own position and my defence; though, perhaps, in a civil war, I might fairly go further in opposition. I could not, with my convictions, vote men and money for this war, and I would not, as a

Representative, vote against them. I meant that, without opposition, the President might take all the men and all the money he should demand, and then to hold him to a strict accountability before the people for the results. Not believing the soldiers responsible for the war, or its purposes, or its consequences, I have never withheld my vote where their separate interests were concerned. But I have denounced from the beginning the usurpations and the infractions, one and all, of law and Constitution, by the President and those under him; their repeated and persistent arbitrary arrests, the suspension of *habeas corpus*, the violation of freedom of the mails, of the private house, of the press, and of speech, and all the other multiplied wrongs and outrages upon public liberty and private right, which have made this country one of the worst despotisms on earth for the past twenty months; and I will continue to rebuke and denounce them to the end; and the people, thank God, have at last heard and heeded, and rebuked them, too. To the record and to time I appeal again for my justification.

And now, sir, I recur to the state of the Union to-day. What is it? Sir, twenty months have elapsed, but the rebellion is not crushed out; its military power has not been broken; the insurgents have not dispersed. The Union is not restored, nor the Constitution maintained, nor the laws enforced. Twenty, sixty, ninety, three hundred, six hundred days have passed; a thousand millions been expended, and three hundred thousand lives lost, or bodies mangled; and to-day the Confederate flag is still near the Potomac and the Ohio, and the Confederate Government stronger, many times, than at the beginning. Not a State has been restored, not any part of any State has voluntarily returned to the Union. And has anything been wanting that Congress, or the States, or the people

M

in their most generous enthusiasm, their most impassioned patriotism, could bestow? Was it power? And did not the party of the Executive control the entire Federal Government, every State Government, every county, every city, town, and village in the North and West? Was it patronage? All belonged to it. Was it influence? What more? Did not the school, the college, the church, the press, the secret orders, the municipality, the corporation, railroads, telegraphs, express companies, the voluntary association, all, all yield it to the utmost? Was it unanimity? Never was an administration so supported in England or America. Five men and half a score of newspapers made up the opposition. Was it enthusiasm? The enthusiasm was fanatical. There has been nothing like it since the Crusades. Was it confidence? Sir, the faith of the people exceeded that of the patriarch. They gave up Constitution, law, right, liberty, all at your demand for arbitrary power, that the rebellion might, as you promised, be crushed out in three months, and the Union restored. Was credit needed? You took control of a country, young, vigorous, and inexhaustible in wealth and resources, and of a Government almost free from public debt, and whose good faith had never been tarnished. Your great national loan-bubble failed miserably, as it deserved to fail; but the bankers and merchants of Philadelphia, New York, and Boston lent you more than their entire banking capital. And when that failed, too, you forced credit, by declaring your paper promises to pay a legal tender for all debts. Was money wanted? You had all the revenues of the United States, diminished indeed, but still in gold. The whole wealth of the country, to the last dollar, lay at your feet. Private individuals, municipal corporations, the State Governments, all in their frenzy gave you money or means with reckless prodigality. The great Eastern cities lent you $150,000,000. Congress voted, first, the sum of $250,000,000, and next $500,000,000 more in loans; and then, first, $50,000,000, then $10,000,000, next $90,000,000, and, in July last, $150,000,000 in Treasury notes; and the Secretary has issued also a "paper postage currency," in sums as low as five cents, limited in amount only by his discretion. Nay, more; already since the 4th of July, 1861, this House has appropriated $2,400,000,000, almost every dollar without debate, and without a recorded vote. A thousand millions have been expended since the 15th of April, 1861; and a public debt or liability of $1,500,000,000 already incurred. And, to support all this stupendous outlay and indebtedness, a system of taxation, direct and indirect, has been inaugurated the most onerous and unjust ever imposed upon any but a conquered people.

Money and credit, then, you have had in prodigal profusion. And were men wanted? More than a million rushed to arms! Seventy-five thousand first (and the country stood aghast at the multitude), then eighty-three thousand more were demanded; and three hundred and ten thousand responded to the call. The President next asked for four hundred thousand, and Congress, in its generous confidence, gave him five hundred thousand; and, not to be outdone, he took six hundred and thirty-seven thousand. Half of these melted away in their first campaign; and the President demanded three hundred thousand more for the war, and then drafted yet another three hundred thousand for nine months. The fabled hosts of Xerxes had been outnumbered. And yet victory strangely follows the standards of the foe. From Great Bethel to Vicksburg, the battle has not been to the strong. Yet every disaster, except the last, has been followed by a call for more troops, and every time so far they have been promptly furnished. From the beginning the war has been conducted like a political campaign, and it has been the folly of the party in power that they have assumed that numbers alone would win the field in a contest not with ballots, but with musket and sword. But numbers you have had almost without number—the largest, best appointed, best armed, fed, and clad, host of brave men, well organised and disciplined ever marshalled. A navy, too, not the most formidable, perhaps, but the most numerous and gallant, and the costliest in the world, and against a foe almost without a navy at all. Twenty million people, and every element of strength and force at command—power, patronage, influence, unanimity, enthusiasm, confidence, credit, money, men, an army and a navy the largest and the noblest ever set in the field or afloat upon the sea; with the support, almost servile, of every State, county, and municipality in the North and West; with a Congress swift to do the bidding of the Executive; without opposition anywhere at home, and with an arbitrary power which neither the Czar of Russia nor the Emperor of Austria dare exercise; yet, after nearly two years of more vigorous prosecution of war than ever recorded in history; after more skirmishes, combats, and battles than Alexander, Cæsar, or the first Napoleon ever fought in any five years of their military career, you have utterly, signally, disastrously—I will not say ignominiously—failed to subdue ten millions of "rebels," whom you had taught the people of the North and West not only to hate but to despise. Rebels, did I say. Yes; your fathers were rebels, or your grandfathers. He who now before me on canvas looks down so sadly upon us, the false, degenerate, and imbecile guardians of the great Republic which he founded, was a rebel. And yet we, cradled ourselves in rebellion, and who have fostered and

fraternised with every insurrection in the nineteenth century everywhere throughout the globe, would now, for-
sooth, make the word "rebel" a reproach. Rebels certainly they are; but all the persistent and stupendous
efforts of the most gigantic warfare of modern times have,
through your incompetency and folly, availed nothing to
crush them out, cut off though they have been by your
blockade from all the world, and dependent only upon
their own courage and resources. And yet they were to
be utterly conquered and subdued in six weeks, or three
months! Sir, my judgment was made up and expressed
from the first. I learned it from Chatham: "My Lords,
you cannot conquer America." And you have not conquered the South. You never will. It is not in the
nature of things possible : much less under your auspices.
But money you have expended without limit, and blood
poured out like water; defeat, debt, taxation, sepulchres,
these are your trophies. In vain the people gave you
treasure and the soldier yielded up his life. "Fight, tax,
emancipate, let these," said the gentleman from Maine
(Mr. Pike), at the last session, "be the trinity of our
salvation." Sir, they have become the trinity of your
deep damnation. The war for the Union is, in your
hands, a most bloody and costly failure. The President
confessed it on the 22nd of September, solemnly, officially,
and under the broad seal of the United States. And he
has now repeated the confession. The priests and rabbis
of abolition taught him that God would not prosper such
a cause. War for the Union was abandoned; war for the
negro openly begun, and with stronger battalions than
before. With what success? Let the dead at Fredericks-
burg and Vickburg answer.

And now, sir, can this war continue? Whence the
money to carry it on? Where the men? Can you

borrow? From whom? Can you tax more? Will the people bear it? Wait till you have collected what is already levied. How many millions more of "legal tender"—to-day forty-one per cent. below the par of gold —can you float? Will men enlist now at any price? Ah, sir, it is easier to die at home—I beg pardon; but I trust I am not "discouraging enlistments." If I am, then first arrest Lincoln, Stanton, and Halleck, and some of your other Generals, and I will retract; yes, I will recant. But can you draft again? Ask New England—New York. Ask Massachusetts. Where are the nine hundred thousand? Ask not Ohio—the North-west. She thought you were in earnest, and gave you all, all—more than you demanded.

> " The wife whose babe first smiled that day,
> The fair, fond bride of yester eve,
> And aged sire and matron grey,
> Saw the loved warriors haste away,
> And deemed it sin to grieve."

Sir, in blood she has atoned for her credulity; and now there is mourning in every house, and distress and sadness in every heart. Shall she give you any more?

But ought this war to continue? I answer—No, not a day, not an hour. What then? Shall we separate? Again I answer—No, no, no! What then? And now, sir, I come to the grandest and most solemn problem of statesmanship from the beginning of time; and to the God of heaven, illuminer of hearts and minds, I would humbly appeal for some measure, at least, of light and wisdom and strength to explore and reveal the dark but possible future of this land.

Can the Union of these States be Restored? How shall it be done?

And why not? Is it historically impossible? Sir, the frequent civil wars and conflicts between the States of

Greece did not prevent their cordial union to resist the Persian invasion; nor did even the thirty years' Peloponnesian war, springing in part from the abduction of slaves, and embittered and disastrous as it was—let Thucidides speak—wholly destroy the fellowship of those States. The wise Romans ended the three years' social war after many bloody battles, and much atrocity, by admitting the States of Italy to all the rights and privileges of Roman citizenship—the very object to secure which these States had taken up arms. The border wars between Scotland and England, running through centuries, did not prevent the final union, in peace and by adjustment, of the two kingdoms under one monarch. Compromise did at last what ages of coercion and attempted conquest had failed to effect. England kept the crown, while Scotland gave the king to wear it; and the memories of Wallace and the Bruce of Bannockburn became part of the glories of British history.

*   *   *   *   *

Sir, the rivalries of the Houses of York and Lancaster filled all England with cruelty and slaughter; yet compromise and intermarriage ended the strife at last, and the white rose and the red were blended in one. Who dreamed a month before the death of Cromwell that in two years the people of England, after twenty years of civil war and usurpation, would, with great unanimity, restore the House of Stuart in the person of its most worthless Prince, whose father but eleven years before they had beheaded? And who could have foretold in the beginning of 1812, that, within some three years, Napoleon would be in exile upon a desert island, and the Bourbons restored? Armed foreign intervention did it; but it is a strange history. Or who then expected to see a nephew of Napoleon, thirty-five years later, with the consent of the people, supplant the Bourbon, and reign Emperor of France? Sir, many States and people, once separate, have become united in the course of ages through natural causes and without conquest; but I remember a single instance only in history of States or people once united, and speaking the same language, who have been forced permanently asunder by civil strife or war, unless they were separated by distance or vast natural boundaries. The secession of the Ten Tribes is the exception: these parted without actual war.

*   *   *   *   *   *

But when Moses, the greatest of all statesmen, would secure a distinct nationality and government to the Hebrews, he left Egypt and established his people in a distant country. In modern times, the Netherlands, three centuries ago, won their independence by the sword; but France and the English channel separated them from Spain. So did our thirteen Colonies; but the Atlantic Ocean divorced us from England. So did Mexico, and other Spanish colonies in America; but the same ocean divided them from Spain. Cuba and the Canadas still adhere to the parent government. And who now, North or South, in Europe or America, looking into history, shall presumptuously say that because of civil war the reunion of these States is impossible? War, indeed, while it lasts is disunion, and, if it lasts long enough, will be final, eternal separation first, and anarchy and despotism afterward. Hence I would hasten peace now, to-day, by every honorable appliance.

*   *   *   *   *   *

But if disunionists in the East will force a separation of any of these States, and a boundary line purely conventional, is at last to be marked out, it must and it will be either from Lake Erie upon the shortest line to the Ohio River, or from Manhattan to the Canadas.

And now, sir, is there any difference of race here, so radical as to forbid reunion? I do not refer to the negro race, styled now, in unctuous official phrase by the President, "Americans of African descent." Certainly, sir, there are two white races in the United States, both from the same common stock, and yet so distinct—one of them so peculiar—that they develop different forms of civilization, and might belong, almost, to different types of mankind. But the boundary of these two races is not at all marked by the line which divides the slaveholding from the non-slaveholding States. If race is to be the geographical limit of disunion, then Mason and Dixon's can never be the line.

* * * * * *

And now, sir, I propose to briefly consider the causes which led to disunion and the present civil war; and to inquire whether they are eternal and ineradicable in their nature, and at the same time powerful enough to overcome all the causes and considerations which impel to reunion.

Having two years ago discussed fully and elaborately the more abstruse and remote causes whence civil commotions in all governments, and those also which are peculiar to our complex and Federal system, such as the consolidating tendencies of the general government, because of executive power and patronage, and of the tariff, and taxation, and disbursement generally, all unjust and burdensome to the West equally with the South, I pass them by now.

What, then, I ask, is the immediate, direct cause of disunion and this civil war? Slavery, it is answered.

Sir, that is the philosophy of the rustic in the play—
"that a great cause of the night, is lack of the sun."
Certainly, slavery was in one sense—very obscure, indeed
—the cause of the war. Had there been no slavery here,
this particular war about slavery would never have been
waged. In a like sense, the Holy Sepulchre was the cause
of the war of the Crusades; and had Troy or Carthage
never existed, there never would have been Trojan or
Carthagenian war, and no such personages as Hector and
Hannibal; and no Iliad or Æneid would have been
written. But far better say that the negro is the cause of
the war; for had there been no negro here, there would
be no war just now. What then? Exterminate him?
Who demands it? Colonize him? How? Where? When?
At whose cost? Sir, let us have an end of this folly.

But slavery is the cause of the war. Why? Because
the South obstinately and wickedly refused to restrict or
abolish it at the demand of the philosophers or fanatics
and demagogues of the North and West. Then, sir, it
was abolition, the purpose to abolish or interfere with and
hem in slavery, which caused disunion and war. Slavery
is only the subject, but abolition the cause, of this civil
war. It was the persistent and determined agitation in
the free States of the question of abolishing slavery in the
South, because of the alleged "irrepressible conflict" between the forms of labour in the two sections, or in the
false and mischievous cant of the day, between freedom
and slavery, that forced a collision of arms at last. Sir,
that conflict was not confined to the Territories. It was
expressly proclaimed by its apostles, as between the States
also, against the institution of domestic slavery everywhere.
But, assuming the platforms of the Republican Party as
the standard, and stating the case most strongly in favour
of that party, it was the refusal of the South to consent

that slavery should be excluded from the Territories that led to the continued agitation, North and South, of that question, and finally to disunion and civil war. Sir, I will not be answered now by the old clamour about "the aggressions of the slave power." That miserable spectre, that unreal mockery, has been exorcised and expelled by debt and taxation and blood. If that power did govern this country for the sixty years preceding this terrible revolution, then the sooner this Administration and Government return to the principles and policy of Southern statesmanship, the better for the country; and that, Sir, is already, or soon will be, the judgment of the people. But I deny that it was the "slave-power" that governed for so many years, and so wisely and well. It was the Democratic Party, and its principles and policy, moulded and controlled, indeed, largely by Southern statesmen. Neither will I be stopped by that other cry of mingled fanaticism and hypocrisy, about the sin and barbarism of African slavery. Sir, I see more of barbarism and sin, a thousand times, in the continuance of this war, the dissolution of the Union, the breaking up of this Government, and the enslavement of the white race by debt and taxes and arbitrary power. The day of fanatics and sophists and enthusiasts, thank God, is gone at last; and though the age of chivalry may not, the age of practical statesmanship is about to return. Sir, I accept the language and intent of the Indiana resolution to the full— " that in considering terms of settlement we will look only to the welfare, peace, and safety of the white race, without reference to the effect that settlement may have upon the condition of the African." And when we have done this, my word for it, the safety, peace, and welfare of the African will have been best secured. Sir, there is fifty-fold less of anti-slavery sentiment to-day in the West than there was two years ago; and, if this war be continued, there will be still less a year hence. The people there begin, at last, to comprehend that domestic slavery in the South is a question, not of morals, or religion, or humanity, but a form of labour, perfectly compatible with the dignity of free white labour in the same community, and with national vigour, power, and prosperity, and especially with military strength. They have learned, or begin to learn, that the evils of the system affect the master alone, or the community and State in which it exists; and that we of the free States partake of all the material benefits of the institution, unmixed with any part of its mischiefs. They believe, also, in the subordination of the negro race to the white where they both exist together, and that the condition of the subordination, as established in the South, is far better every way for the negro than the hard servitude of poverty, degradation, and crime to which he is subjected in the free States. All this, Sir, may be " proslaveryism," if there be such a word. Perhaps it is; but the people of the West now begin to think it wisdom and good sense. We will not establish slavery in our own midst, neither will we abolish or interfere with it outside of our own limits.

Sir, an anti-slavery paper in New York (the "Tribune"), the most influential, and, therefore, most dangerous of all that class—it would exhibit more of dignity, and command more of influence, if it were always to discuss public questions and public men with a decent respect—laying aside now the epithets of " secessionists" and " traitor," has returned to its ancient political nomenclature, and calls certain members of this House " pro-slavery." Well, Sir, in the old sense of the term as applied to the Democratic party, I will not object. I said years ago, and it is a fitting time now to repeat it :—

"If to love my country; to cherish the Union; to revere the Constitution; if to abhor the madness and hate the treason which would lift up a sacrilegious hand against either; if to read that in the past, to behold it in the present, to foresee it in the future of this land, which is of more value to us and to the world for ages to come than all the multiplied millions who have inhabited Africa from the Creation to this day!—if this is to be pro-slavery, then is every nerve, fibre, vein, bone, tendon, joint, and ligament, from the topmost hair of the head to the last extremity of the foot, I am all over and altogether a pro-slavery man."

And now, sir, I come to the great and controlling question within which the whole question of union or disunion is bound up. Is there "an irrepressible conflict" between the slaveholding and the non-slaveholding States? Must "the cotton and rice-fields of South Carolina and the sugar-plantations of Louisiana," in the language of Mr. Seward, "be ultimately tilled by free labour, and Charleston and New Orleans become marts for legitimate merchandise alone, or else the rye-fields and wheat-fields of Massachusetts and New York again be surrendered by their farmers to slave culture and the production of slaves, and Boston and New York become once more markets for trade in the bodies and souls of men?" If so, then there is an end of all union and for ever. You cannot abolish slavery by the sword; still less by proclamations, though the President were to "proclaim" every month. Of what possible avail was his proclamation of September? Did the South submit? Was she even alarmed? And yet he has now fulminated another "bull against the comet"— *brutum fulmen*—and, threatening servile insurrection with all its horrors, has yet coolly appealed to the judgment of mankind, and invoked the blessing of the God of peace and love! But declaring it a military necessity, an essential measure of war to subdue the rebels, yet, with admirable wisdom, he expressly exempts from incorporation the only States and parts of States in the South where he has the military power to execute it.

Neither, sir, can you abolish slavery by argument. As well attempt to abolish marriage or the relation of paternity. The South is resolved to maintain it at every hazard and by every sacrifice; and if "this Union cannot endure part slave and part free," then it is already and finally dissolved. Talk not to me of "West Virginia." Tell me not of Missouri, trampled under the feet of your soldiery. * * * * Sir, the destiny of those States must abide the issue of the war. But Kentucky you may find tougher. And Maryland—

"Even in their ashes live their wonted fires."

Nor will Delaware be found wanting in the day of trial.

But I deny the doctrine. It is full of disunion and civil war, it is disunion itself. Whoever first taught it ought to be dealt with as not only hostile to the Union, but an enemy of the human race. Sir, the fundamental idea of the Constitution is the perfect and eternal compatibility of a union of States "part slave and part free;" else the Constitution never would have been framed, nor the Union founded: and seventy years of successful experiment have approved the wisdom of the plan. In my deliberate judgment, a Confederacy made up of slaveholding and non-slaveholding States is, in the nature of things, the strongest of all popular Governments. African slavery has been, and is, eminently conservative. It makes the absolute political equality of the white race everywhere practicable. It dispenses with the English order of nobility, and leaves every white man, North and South, owning slaves or owning none, the equal of every other white man. It has reconciled universal suffrage throughout the free States with the stability of Government. I speak not now of its material benefits to the

North and West, which are many and more obvious. But the South, too, has profited in many ways by a union with the non-slaveholding States. Enterprise, industry, self-reliance, perseverance, and the other hardy virtues of a people living in a higher latitude and without hereditary servants, she has learned or received from the North. Sir, it is easy, I know, to denounce all this, and to revile him who utters it. Be it so. The English is, of all languages, the most copious in words of bitterness and reproach. " Pour on: I will endure."

Then, sir, there is not an " irrepressible conflict " between slave labour and free labour. There is no conflict at all. Both exist together in perfect harmony in the South. The master and the slave, the white labourer and the black, work together in the same field or the same shop, and without the slightest sense of degradation. They are not equals, either socially or politically. And why not, then, cannot Ohio, having only free labour, live in harmony with Kentucky, which has both slave and free? Above all, why cannot Massachusetts allow the same right of choice to South Carolina, separated as they are a thousand miles, by other States who would keep the peace and live in good will? Why this civil war? Whence disunion? Not from slavery—not because the South chooses to have two kinds of labour instead of one; but from *sectionalism*—always and everywhere a disintegrating principle. Sectional jealousy and hate,— these, sir, are the only elements of conflict between these States, and, though powerful they are yet not at all irrepressible. They exist between families, communities, towns, cities, counties, and States; and if not repressed would dissolve all society and government. They exist also between other sections than the North and South. Sectionalism East, many years ago, saw the South and

West united by the ties of geographical position, migra-
tion, intermarriage, and interest; and thus strong enough
to control the power and policy of the Union. It found
us divided only by different forms of labour; and, with
consummate but most guilty sagacity, it seized upon the
question of slavery as the surest and most powerful
instrumentality by which to separate the West from the
South, and bind her wholly to the North. Encouraged
every way from abroad by those who were jealous of our
prosperity and greatness, and who knew the secret of our
strength, it proclaimed the "irrepressible conflict" between slave labour and free labour. It taught the people
of the North to forget both their duty and their interests;
and, aided by the artificial ligaments and influence which
money and enterprise had created between the sea-board
and the North-west, it persuaded the people of that
section, also, to yield up every tie which binds them to
the great Valley of the Mississippi, and to join their
political fortunes especially wholly with the East. It
resisted the fugitive slave law, and demanded the exclusion
of slavery from all the Territories and from this District,
and clamoured against the admission of any more slave
States into the Union. It organised a sectional anti-
slavery party, and thus drew to its aid as well political
ambition and interest as fanaticism; and after twenty-five
years of incessant and vehement agitation, it obtained
possession finally, and upon that issue, of the Federal
Government and of every State Government North and
West. And to-day, we are in the midst of the greatest,
most cruel, most destructive civil war ever waged. But
two years, sir, of blood and debt and taxation and incipient commercial ruin are teaching the people of the West,
and I trust of the North also, the folly and madness of
this crusade against African slavery, and the wisdom and

necessity of a union of the States, as our fathers made it, "part slave and part free."

*   *   *   *   *

What, then, sir, with so many causes impelling to reunion, keeps us apart to-day? Hate, passion, antagonism, revenge, all heated seven times hotter by war. Sir, these, while they last, are the most powerful of all motives with a people, and with the individual man; but fortunately they are the least durable. They hold a divided sway in the same bosoms with the nobler qualities of love, justice, reason, placability; and, except when at their height, are weaker than the sense of interest, and always, in States at least, give way to it at last. No statesman who yields himself up to them can govern wisely or well; and no State whose policy is controlled by them can either prosper or endure. But war is both their offspring and their aliment, and, while it lasts, all other motives are subordinate. The virtues of peace cannot flourish, cannot even find development in the midst of fighting; and this civil war keeps in motion the centrifugal forces of the Union, and gives to them increased strength and activity every day. But such, and so many and powerful, in my judgment, are the cementing or centripetal agencies impelling us together that nothing but perpetual war and strife can keep us always divided.

Sir, I do not under-estimate the power of the prejudices of section, or, what is much stronger, of race. Prejudice is colder, and, therefore, more durable than the passions of hate and revenge, or the spirit of antagonism. But, as I have already said, its boundary in the United States is not Mason and Dixon's line. The long standing mutual jealousies of New England and the South do not primarily grow out of slavery. They are deeper, and will always be the chief obstacle in the way of full and abso-

N

lute reunion.   They are founded in difference of manners,
habits, and social life, and different opinions about politics,
morals, and religion.   Sir, after all, this whole war is not
so much one of sections—least of all, between the slaveholding and non-slaveholding sections— as of races, representing not difference in blood, but mind and its development, and different types of civilization.   It is the old
conflict of the Cavalier and the Roundhead, the Liberalist
and the Puritan ; or rather it is a conflict upon new issues
of the ideas and elements represented by those names.
It is a war of the Yankee and the Southron.   Said a
Boston writer the other day, eulogising a New England
officer who fell at Fredericksburgh : " This is Massachusets' war ; Massachusets and South Carolina made it."
But in the beginning, the Roundhead outwitted the
Cavalier, and by a skilful use of slavery and the negro
united all New England first, and afterward the entire
North and West, and finally sent out to battle against
him Celt and Saxon, German and Knickerbocker, Catholic
and Episcopalian, and even a part of his own household
and of the descendants of his own stock.   Said Mr. Jefferson, when New England threatened secession some sixty
years ago : "No, let us keep the Yankees to quarrel with."
Ah, sir, he forgot that quarrelling is always a hazardous
experiment; and, after some time, the countrymen of
Adams proved themselves too sharp at that work for the
countrymen of Jefferson.   But every day the contest now
tends again to its natural and original elements.   In many
parts of the North-west—I might add of Pennsylvania,
New Jersey, and New York city—the prejudice against
the " Yankee " has always been almost as bitter as in the
South.   Suppressed for a little while by the anti-slavery
sentiment and the war, it threatens now to break forth in
one of those great and popular uprisings, in the midst of

which reason and justice are for the time utterly silenced. I speak advisedly; and let New England heed, else she, and the whole East, too, in their struggle for power, may learn yet from the West the same lesson which civil war taught to Rome, that *evulgato imperii* arcano posse, principem alibi, quam Romæ fieri.* The people of the West demand peace, and they begin to more than suspect that New England is in the way. The storm rages ; and they believe that she, not slavery, is the cause. The ship is sore tried; and passengers and crew are now almost ready to propitiate the waves by throwing the ill-omened prophet overboard. In plain English—not very classic, but most expressive—they threaten to " set New England out in the cold."

And now, sir, I, who have not a drop of New England blood in my veins, but was born in Ohio, and am solely of Southern ancestry—with a slight cross of Pennsylvania Scotch-Irish—would speak a word to the men of the West and the South, in behalf of New England.

*　*　*　*　*　*

Sir, they who would exclude New England in any reconstruction of the Union, assume that all New Englanders are "Yankees" and Puritans; and that the Puritan or pragmatical element, or type of civilization, has always held undisputed sway. Well, sir, Yankees, certainly, they are in one sense; and so, to Old England, we are all Yankees, North and South; and to the South, just now, or a little while ago, we of the Middle and Western States, also, are, or were, Yankees too. But there is really a very large and most liberal and conservative non-Puritan element in the population of New England, which, for many years, struggled for the mastery, and sometimes held it. It divided Maine, New Hampshire, and Connecticut, and once controlled Rhode Island wholly. It held the sway

during the Revolution, and at the period when the Constitution was founded, and for some years afterward.
Mr. Calhoun said very justly, in 1847, that to the wisdom
and enlarged patriotism of Sherman and Ellsworth, on the
slavery question, we were indebted for this admirable
Government, and that, along with Patterson, of New
Jersey, " their names ought to be engraven on brass, and
live for ever." And Mr. Webster, in 1830, in one of
those grand historic word-paintings, in which he was so
great a master, said of Massachusets and South Carolina:
" Hand in hand they stood around the administration of
Washington, and felt his own great arm lean on them for
support." Indeed, sir, it was not till some thirty years
ago, that the narrow, presumptuous, intermeddling, and
fanatical spirit of the old Puritan element began to re-
appear in a form very much more aggressive and destructive
than at first, and threatened to obtain absolute mastery in
church, and school, and State. A little earlier it had
struggled hard, but the conservatives proved too strong
for it, and so long as the great statesmen and jurists of
the Whig and Democratic parties survived, it made but
small progress, though John Quincy Adams gave to it the
strength of his great name. But after their death it broke
in as a flood, and swept away the last vestige of the ancient,
liberal, and tolerating conservatism. Then, every form
and development of fanaticism sprang up in rank and most
luxuriant growth, till Abolitionism, the chief fungus of all,
overspread the whole of New England first, and then the
Middle States, and finally, every State in the North-west.

Certainly, sir, the more liberal or non-Puritan element
was mainly, though not altogether, from the old Puritan
stock, or largely crossed with it. But even within the
first ten years after the landing of the Pilgrims, a more
enlarged and tolerating civilization was introduced. Roger

Williams, not of the " Mayflower," though a Puritan himself, and thoroughly imbued with all its peculiarities of
cant and creed and form of worship, seems yet to have
had naturally a more liberal spirit; and, first, perhaps, of
all men, some three or more years before " The Ark and
the Dove" touched the shores of the St. Mary's, in Maryland, taught the sublime doctrine of toleration of opinion
and practice in religion.   Threatened, first, with banish-
ment to England, so as to " remove as far as possible the
infection of his principles;" and afterwards actually banished
beyond the jurisdiction of Massachusets, because, in the
language of the sentence of the General Court, " he
broached and divulged divers new and strange doctrines
against the authority of magistrates," over the religious
opinions of men, thereby disturbing the peace of the
colony.   He became the founder of Rhode Island, and,
indeed, of a large part of New England society; and,
whether from his teaching and example, and in the persons
of his descendants and those of his associates, or from
other causes, and another stock, there has always been a
large infusion throughout New England of what may be
called the Roger Williams' element, as distinguished from
the extreme Puritan, or Mayflower and Plymouth Rock
type of the New Englander; and its influence, till late
years, has always been powerful.

Sir, I would not deny or disparage the austere virtues
of the old Puritans of England or America; but I do
believe that, in the very nature of things, no community
could exist long in peace, and no Government endure
long alone, or become great, where that element in its
earliest or its more recent form holds supreme control.
And it is my solemn conviction that there can be no
possible or durable reunion of these States until it shall
have been again subordinated to other and more liberal

and conservative elements, and, above all, until its worst and most mischievous development, abolitionism, has been utterly extinguished. Sir, the peace of the Union and of this continent demands it. But, fortunately, those very elements exist abundantly in New England herself; and to her I look with confidence to secure to them the mastery within her limits. In fact, sir, the true voice of New England has for some years past been but rarely heard here or elsewhere in public affairs. Men now control her politics and are in high places, State and Federal, who, twenty years ago, could not have been chosen as select men in old Massachusets. But let her remember at last her ancient renown; let her turn from vain-glorious admiration of the stone monuments of her heroes and patriots of a former age, to generous emulation of the noble and manly virtues which they were designed to commemorate. Let us hear less from her of the Pilgrim Fathers and the Mayflower and of Plymouth Rock, and more of Roger Williams and his compatriots and his toleration. Let her banish now and for ever her dreamers and her sophists and her fanatics, and call back again into her State Administration and into the national councils "her men of might, her grand in soul,"—some of them still live,—and she will yet escape the dangers which now threaten her with isolation.

Then, sir, while I am inexorably hostile to Puritan domination in religion or literature or politics, I am not in favour of the proposed exclusion of New England. I would have the union as it was; and, first, New England as she was. But if New England will have no Union with slaveholders—if she is not content with "the Union as it was"—then upon her own head be the responsibility for secession. And there will be no more coercion now. I, at least, will be exactly consistent.

And now, sir, can the central States, New York, New Jersey, and Pennsylvania, consent to separation? Can New York city? Sir, the trade of the South made her largely what she is. She was the factor and the banker of the South—cotton filled her harbour with shipping and her banks with gold; but in an evil hour the foolish—I will not say bad—" men of Gotham " persuaded her merchant princes—against their first lesson in business— that she could retain or force back the Southern trade by war. War, indeed, has given her just now a new business and trade greater and more profitable than the old; but, ` with disunion, that too must perish. And let not Wall Street, or any other great interest, mercantile, manufacturing, or commercial, imagine that it shall have power enough or wealth enough to stand in the way of reunion through peace. Let them learn, one and all, that a public man who has the people as his support is stronger than they, though he may not be worth a million nor even one dollar. A little while ago the banks said that they were king, but President Jackson speedily taught them their mistake. Next, railroads assumed to be king; and cotton once vaunted largely his kingship. Sir, these are only of the royal family—princes of the blood. There is but one king on earth.

But to return. New Jersey, too, is bound closely to the South, and the South to her; and more and longer than any other State, she remembered both her duty to the Constitution and her interest in the Union. And Pennsylvania, a sort of middle ground, just between the North and the South, and extending, also, to the West, is united by nearer, if not stronger ties, to every section, than any other one State, unless it be Ohio. She was— she is yet—the keystone in the great but now crumbling arch of the Union. She is a border State; and, more

than that, she has less within her of the fanatical or disturbing element than any of the States. The people of
Pennsylvania are quiet, peaceable, practical, and enterprising, without being aggressive. They have more of the
honest old English and German thrift than any other. No
people mind more diligently their own business. They
have but one idiosyncrasy or specialty—the tariff; and
even that is really far more a matter of tradition than of
substantial interest. The industry, enterprise, and thrift
of Pennsylvania are abundantly able to take care of themselves against any competition. In any event, the Union
is of more value, many times, to her than any local
interest.

But other ties also bind these States—Pennsylvania
and New Jersey, especially—to the South, and the South
to them. Only an imaginary line separates the former
from Delaware and Maryland. The Delaware River,
common to both Pennsylvania and New Jersey, flows into
Delaware Bay. The Susquehanna empties its waters,
through Pennsylvania and Maryland, into the Chesapeake.
And that great watershed itself, extending to Norfolk, and,
therefore, almost to the North Carolina line, does belong,
and must ever belong, in common to the Central and
Southern States, under one Government; or else the line
of separation will be the Potomac to its head waters. All
of Delaware and Maryland, and the counties of Accomac
and Northampton, in Virginia, would, in that event, follow
the fortunes of the Northern Confederacy! In fact, sir,
disagreeable as the idea may be to many within their limits
on both sides, no man who looks at the map and then
reflects upon history and the force of natural causes, and
considers the present actual and the future probable position of the hostile armies and navies at the end of this
war, ought for a moment to doubt that either the States

and counties which I have named must go with the North, or Pennsylvania and New Jersey with the South. Military force on either side cannot control the destiny of the States lying between the mouth of the Chesapeake and the Hudson. And if that bay were itself made the line, Delaware, and the eastern shore of Maryland and Virginia, would belong to the North; while Norfolk, the only capacious harbour on the South-eastern coast, must be commanded by the guns of some new fortress upon Cape Charles; and Baltimore, the now queenly city, seated upon the very boundary of two rival, yes, hostile, Confederacies, would rapidly fall into decay.

And now, Sir, I will not ask whether the North-west can consent to separation from the South. Never. Nature forbids. We are only a part of the great Valley of the Mississippi. There is no line of latitude upon which to separate. The South would not desire the old line of 36° 36' on both sides of the river; and there is no natural boundary east and west. The nearest to it are the Ohio and Missouri rivers. But that line would leave Cincinnati and St. Louis, as border cities, like Baltimore, to decay, and, extending fifteen hundred miles in length, would become the scene of an eternal border war-fare without example even in the worst of times. Sir, we cannot, ought not, will not, separate from the South. And if you of the East, who have found this war against the South and for the negro, gratifying to your hate, profitable to your purse, will continue it till a separation be forced between the slaveholding and your non-slaveholding States, then, believe me, and accept it, as you did not the other solemn warnings of years past, the day which divides the North from the South, that self-same day decrees eternal divorce between the West and the East.

Sir, our destiny is fixed. There is not one drop of rain, which, descending from the heavens and fertilizing our soil, causes it to yield an abundant harvest, but flows into the Mississippi, and there, mingling with the waters of that mighty river, finds its way, at last, to the Gulf of Mexico. And we must and will follow it with travel and trade, not by treaty, but by right, freely, peaceably, and without restriction or tribute, under the same government and flag, to its home in the bosom of that gulf. Sir, we will not remain, after separation from the South, a province or appanage of the East, to bear her burdens and pay her taxes; nor hemmed in and isolated as we are, and without a sea coast, could we long remain a distinct confederacy. But wherever we go, married to the South or to the East, we bring with us three-fourths of the territories of that valley to the Rock Mountains, and it may be to the Pacific—the grandest and most magnificent dowry which bride ever had to bestow. Behold to-day two separate governments in one country, and without a natural dividing line ; with two Presidents and Cabinets, and a double Congress ; and yet each under a constitution so exactly similar, the one to the other, that a stranger could scarce discern the difference. Was ever folly and madness like this ? Sir, it is not in the nature of things that it should so continue long.

But why speak of ways or terms of reunion now? The will is yet wanting in both sections. Union is consent and good will and fraternal affection. War is force, hate, revenge. Is the country tired at last of war ? Has the experiment been tried long enough ? Has sufficient blood been shed, treasure expended, and misery inflicted in both the North and the South ? What then? Stop fighting. Make an armistice,—no formal treaty. Withdraw your army from the seceded States. Reduce both armies to a fair and sufficient peace establishment. De- clare absolute free trade between the North and South. Buy and sell. Agree upon a zollverein. Recall your fleets. Break up your blockade. Reduce your navy. Restore travel. Open up railroads. Re-establish the telegraph. Reunite your express companies. No more Monitors and iron-clads, but set your friendly steamers and steamships again in motion. Visit the North and West. Visit the South. Exchange newspapers. Mi- grate. Intermarry. Let slavery alone. Hold elections at the appointed times. Choose a new President in sixty- four. And when the gospel of peace shall have descended again from heaven into their hearts, and the gospel of abolition and of hate been expelled, let your clergy and the Churches meet again in Christian intercourse, North and South. Let the secret orders and voluntary associa- tions everywhere reunite as brethren once more. In short, give to all the natural and all the artificial causes which impel us together their fullest sway. Let time do his office—drying tears, dispelling sorrows, mellowing passion, and making herb and grass and tree to grow again upon the hundred battle-fields of this terrible war.

"But this is recognition." It is not formal recogni- tion, to which I will not consent. Recognition now, and attempted permanent treaties about boundary, travel, and trade, and partition of Territories, would end in a war fiercer and more disastrous than before. Recognition is absolute disunion; and not between the slave and the free States, but with Delaware and Maryland as part of the North, and Kentucky and Missouri part of the West. But wherever the actual line, every evil and mischief of disunion is implied in it. And for similar reasons, Sir, I would not at this time press hastily a convention of the States. The men who now would hold seats in such a convention would, upon both sides, if both agreed to attend, come together full of the hate and bitterness inseparable from a civil war. No, Sir; let passion have time to cool, and reason resume its sway. It cost thirty years of desperate and most wicked patience and industry to destroy or impair the magnificent temple of this Union. Let us be content if, within three years, we shall be able to restore it.

But certainly what I propose is informal, practical recognition. And that is precisely what exists to-day, and has existed, more or less defined, from the first. Flags of truce, exchange of prisoners, and all your other observances of the laws, forms, and courtesies of the war are acts of recognition. Sir, does any man doubt to-day that there is a Confederate government at Richmond, and that it is a "belligerent?" Even the Secretary of State has discovered it at last, though he has written ponderous folios of polished rhetoric to prove that it is not. Will continual war, then, without extended and substantial success, make the Confederate States any the ess a government in fact?

" But it confesses disunion." Yes, just as the surgeon, who sets your fractured limb in splints, in order that it may be healed, admits that it is broken. But the government will have failed to " crush out the rebellion." Sir, it has failed. You went to war to prove that we had a government. With what result? To the people of the loyal States it has, in your hands, been the government of King Stork but to the Confederate States, of King Log. " But the rebellion will have triumphed." Better triumph to-day than ten years hence. But I deny it.

The rebellion will at last be crushed out in the only way in which it ever was possible. " But no one will be hung at the end of war." Neither will there be, though the war should last half a century, except by the mob or the hand of arbitrary power. But really, sir, if there is to be no hanging, let this administration, and all who have done its bidding everywhere, rejoice and be exceedingly glad.

And now, sir, allow me a word upon a subject of very great interest at this moment, and most important it may be in its influence upon the future—FOREIGN MEDIATION. I speak not of armed and hostile intervention, which I would resist as long as but one man was left to strike a blow at the invader. But friendly mediation—the kindly offer of an impartial power to stand as a daysman between the contending parties in this most bloody and exhausting strife—ought to be met in a spirit as cordial and ready as that in which it is proffered. It would be churlish to refuse. Certainly, it is not consistent with the former dignity of this government to ask for a mediation; neither, sir, would it befit its ancient magnanimity to reject it. As proposed by the Emperor of France, I would accept it at once. Now is the auspicious moment. It is the speediest, easiest, most graceful mode of sus- pending hostilities. Let us hear no more of the mediation of cannon and the sword. The day for all that has gone by. Let us be statesmen at last. Sir, I give thanks that some, at least, among the republican party seem ready now to lift themselves up to the height of this great argument, and to deal with it in the spirit of the patriots and public men of other countries, and of the better days of the United States.

And now, sir, whatever may have been the motives of England, France, and the other great powers of Europe,

in withholding recognition so long from the Confederate
States, the South and the North are both indebted to
them for a great public service. The south has proved
her ability to maintain herself by her own strength and
resources, without foreign aid, moral or material. And
the North and West—the whole country indeed—these
great powers have served incalculably, by holding back a
solemn proclamation to the world that the Union of these
States was finally and formally dissolved. They have
left to us every motive and every chance for reunion; and
if that has been the purpose of England especially—our
rival so long; interested more than any other in disunion
and the consequent weakening of our great naval and
commercial power, and suffering, too, as she has suffered,
so long and severely because of this war—I do not hesi-
tate to say that she has performed an act of unselfish
heroism without example in history. Was such indeed
her purpose? Let her answer before the impartial
tribunal of posterity. In any event, after the great
reaction in public sentiment in the North and West, to
be followed after some time by a like reaction in the
South, foreign recognition now of the Confederate States
could avail little to delay or prevent final reunion, if, as
I firmly believe, reunion be not only possible but inevitable.

Sir, I have not spoken of foreign arbitration. That is
quite another question. I think it impracticable, and fear
it as dangerous. The very powers,—or any other power,
—which have hesitated to aid disunion directly or by
force, might as authorized arbiters, most readily pronounce for it at last. Very grand, indeed, would be the
tribunal before which the great question of the union of
these States and the final destiny of this continent for

ages would be heard, and historic through all time the ambassadors who should argue it. And if both belligerents consent, let the subjects in controversy be referred to Switzerland, or Russia, or any other impartial and incorruptible power or State in Europe. But at last, sir, the people of these several States here, at home, must be the final arbiter of this great quarrel in America, and the people and States of the North-west the mediators who shall stand, like the prophet, betwixt the living and the dead, that the plague of disunion may be stayed.

Sir, this war, horrible as it is, has taught us all some of the most important and salutary lessons which ever a people learned.

First, it has annihilated, in twenty months, all the false and pernicious theories and teachings of abolitionism for thirty years, and which a mere appeal to facts and argument could not have untaught in half a century. We have learned that the South is not weak, dependent, unenterprising, or corrupted by slavery, luxury, and idleness; but, powerful, earnest, warlike, enduring, self-supporting, full of energy, and inexhaustible in resources. We have been taught, and nowconfess it openly, that African slavery, instead of being a source of weakness to theSouth is one of her main elements of strength; and hence the "military necessity," we are told of abolishing slavery in order to suppress the rebellion. We have learned, also, that the non-slaveholding white men of the South, millions in number, are immovably attached to the institution, and are its chief support; and abolitionists have found out to their infinite surprise and disgust, that the slave is not "panting for freedom," nor pining in silent but revengeful grief over cruelty and oppression inflicted upon him, but happy, contented,

attached deeply to his master, and unwilling—at least not
eager—to accept the precious boon of freedom which they
have proffered him. I appeal to the President for the
proof. I appeal to the fact that fewer slaves have escaped
even from Virginia in now nearly two years than Arnold
and Cornwallis carried away in six months of invasion
in 1781. Finally, sir, we have learned, and the South,
too, what the history of the world ages ago, and our own
history might have taught us, that servile insurrection is
the least of the dangers to which she is exposed. Hence,
in my deliberate judgment, African slavery, as an institution, will come out of this conflict fifty-fold stronger than
when the war began.

The South, too, sir, has learned most important lessons;
and among them, that personal courage is a quality
common to all sections, and that, in battle, the men of
the North, and especially of the West, are their equals.
Hitherto there has been a mutual and most mischievous
mistake upon both sides. The South overvalued its own
personal courage and undervalued ours, and we, too,
readily consented; but at the same time she exaggerated
our aggregate strength and resources, and under-estimated
her own; and we fell into the same error; and hence the
original and fatal mistake or vice of the military policy of
the North, and which has already broken down the war
by its own weight—the belief that we could bring over-
whelming number and power into the field and upon the
sea, and crush out the South at a blow. But twenty
months of terrible warfare have corrected many errors,
and taught us the wisdom of a century. And now, sir,
every one of these lessons will profit us all for ages to
come; and, if we do but reunite, will bind us in a closer,
firmer, more durable union than ever before.

I have now, Mr. Speaker, finished what I desire to say at this time upon the great question of the reunion of these States. I have spoken freely and boldly—not wisely, it may be, for the present, or for myself personally, but most wisely for the future and for my country. Not courting censure, I yet do not shrink from it. My own immediate personal interests, and my chances just now for the more material rewards of ambition, I again surrender as hostages to that great hereafter, the echo of whose footsteps already I hear along the highway of time. Whoever, here or elsewhere, believes that war can restore the Union of these States; whoever would have a war for the abolition of slavery, or disunion; and he who demands Southern independence and final separation, let him speak, for him I have offended. Devoted to the Union from the beginning, I will not desert it now in this the hour of its sorest trial.

Sir, it was the day dream of my boyhood, the cherished desire of my heart in youth, that I might live to see the hundredth anniversary of our national independence, and, as an orator of the day, exult in the expanding glories and greatness of the still United States. That vision lingers yet before my eyes, obscured, indeed, by the cloud and thick darkness and the blood of civil war. But, sir, if the men of this generation are wise enough to profit by the hard experience of the past two years, and will turn their hearts now from bloody intents to the words and art of peace, that day will find us again the United States. And if not earlier, as I would desire and believe, at least upon that day let the great work of reunion be consummated; that thenceforth, for ages, the States and the people who shall fill up this mighty continent, united under one constitution, and in one Union, and the same destiny, shall celebrate it as the birthday both of Independence and of the Great Restoration.

Sir, I repeat it, we are in the midst of the very crisis of this revolution. If to-day we secure peace and begin the work of reunion, we shall yet escape ; if not, I see nothing before us but universal, political, and social revolution, anarchy, and bloodshed, compared with which the Reign of Terror in France was a merciful visitation.

HARRISON AND SONS, PRINTERS, ST. MARTIN'S LANE, W.C.

www.ingramcontent.com/pod-product-compliance
Lightning Source LLC
Chambersburg PA
CBHW030827020726
47499CB00006B/2104